Klytaimnestra
Who Stayed
at Home

Klytaimnestra Who Stayed at Home

NANCY BOGEN

1 9   8 0

The Twickenham Press

NEW YORK

Printing History
Twickenham Press, 1st edition (paperback), 1980
2nd printing...1982   3rd printing...1983
4th printing...1997

Printed in the United States of America
Library of Congress Cataloging in Publication Data

Bogen, Nancy, 1932–
Klytaimnestra Who Stayed at Home.
I. Title.
PZ4.B67435Kl [PS3552.0'434] 813'.54 80-51052

ISBN 0–936726–00–8 (pbk.)

In Memoriam

R I C H M O N D   C O L L E G E

(1 9 6 7 – 7 6)

"Ομηρος καί οἱ τραγωδιογράφοι ἦσαν ψεύσται

Πλάτων

DRAMATIS PERSONAE

(In order of appearance)

An old watchman

His old wife

An old soldier

His granddaughter

The captain of the guard

The stewardess

Elektra,
elder daughter of Klytaimnestra and Agamemnon

Klytaimnestra, the queen

Aigisthos, her lover

High priestess of Hera

Chrysothemis,
younger daughter of Klytaimnestra and Agamemnon

Agamemnon, the king

Kassandra, his Trojan prize

Menon and Lykon, returned heroes

Helen, wife of Epiarchos

The old soldier's son, another returnee

The Day

— I —

Hazy-blue moments before dawn are for sleeping, and the old man's chin had just begun to slap on his chest and his mouth to blow when—look! Specks! There on the horizon!

"At last!"—he hauled himself up and tossed a faggot from his little fire at the heap of dried twigs that he had in readiness hard by.

"*Whoosh!*"—the flames. And—oh Hera—the next instant bright yellow leaps like that were everywhere, on all of the other promontories thereabouts.

"Yes"—there were his pouch with the bread and cheese still untouched in it and almost-full waterskin. I have had a bellyfull of stewing up here—anyone would have who had sat watching thus day in and out like him, that is, ever since some months ago when fires from across the sea had announced the victory. My ass sizzles.

And then he began the long hike down.

Not quite half-way there—"Dizzy, must be going too fast." And he stopped to draw a few breaths, latching on to the branch of an olive tree.

Below him all over it was quiet still. But it would not be

for long, he expected; in a while the roads would be full of people, all of them heading for the shore and the landing place. For so it had passed before when there was a home-coming, in his youth when Atreus was high-king.

He turned toward the water, examining the little black dots really for the first time. Who can it be down there, Agamemnon of Mykenai (son of Atreus) or King Diomedes of Argos?

Oh let it be Agamemnon because then my prize will be bigger. I am entitled to one, I believe; mine was the first fire.

And quite possibly it was indeed Agamemnon, for while there had been no word of him at all since the war ended, Diomedes' ships were known to have been at the mouth of the gulf, but a day's sail away, as long as a month ago. Old Nestor of Pylos and he had parted there after making for home together. So something may have happened to Diomedes. . . .

But onward, I must go onward; at any moment the sun will be up all angry-red, and then my ass will sizzle even more, if that is possible. And so he went on, but more slowly—to save strength; as there might be a long ride in store later, all the way to Mykenai.

Soon, just below him, he made out his small flock of goats —"Hello, my little ones." Then his fig trees, all loaded down but the fruit still puny and hard like boy-balls—"Hee-hee." And through them, their big-leafiness, the straw thatching and mud brick of his hut came into view.

His wife had just lumpishly stepped outside, and as he passed through the gate there she was in her usual place on the ground beside the door doing what she usually did there, winding some strands of wool onto a twig.

"I saw the fires"—this with a dimple for him.

But he had never been one for idle chatter—"Hmm"—

and letting the pouch and skin slip from his hand, hurried on inside to the almost sweet darkness and coolness.

Ah—easing himself down onto his fluffy goatskin mantle. Better—beginning to shed his sweaty rag of a tunic. "Let me have the carafe, will you?"

She padded in and after rummaging around in the back there where they kept things produced it for him. He hefted it—bah, some missing again! Every time my back is turned, it seems. "Been up to your tricks?"

"A little."

A little, a little, a lot. "Water will do just as well; try to remember that."

"Oh." And she padded out again.

He took a pull at it, then another, and then lay back. I will rest up good for now. Then later, when I hear some of them marching down the road—the heroes, their loved ones—I will go out and ask. And if it turns out that they belong to Agamemnon, I will come back for the donkey. If not—

He closed his eyes. It will not be easy getting in at the lower gate there at Mykenai. Well, I will call for the captain of the guard; and when he learns, big man, I would not be surprised if he showed me up to the palace himself.

And once I am there, in the courtyard, the great hall?

Why Agamemnon will be on his throne surrounded by his best men all feasting and drinking. (Large he is too, as I recall, but leaner, bonier.) And when I tell him, he will cry out—"Well done, my good man!" And to the captain—"See that this worthy one has a place and get him something to eat."

And then, ah, the crispy-brown meat the serving men will set before me. And oh, the hot-spicy juices racing from it. I will need a cold goblet to wash it all down.

Then after I have eaten and drunk my fill, they will lead

in an old blind one with long fleecy locks. And he will sing, strumming on his lyre, of how, when Troy fell, Agamemnon, perfect leader, came away with the most splendid of everything from there including the princess Kassandra. And then how after many a weary day on the waves he was greeted by a great leap of flame followed by many lesser ones. And he will liken it all to what happens at twilight— first the evening star appears, then the others.

All strive for but none achieves its crystal-brightness

And when that harper has finished?

Why Agamemnon will send him away with a silver dish.

And then?

And then to me, the worthy watchman, he will present a gold bowl. . . .

Now he would have slept, only all at once his eyes were open again and fastened on the smoke-hole in the ceiling. Or rather it was staring down at him like a sharp warning eye. At the same time there was a voice—"Get up, you, get up!"

What? He sat up, looked around. Who was that?

Again it came—"Get up and go to the beach! Right now—before it is too late!"

Who? What?

He waited for something else, but there was nothing, no more.

Who could it have been? She outside? Playing a new trick? No, it did not sound like her; besides, she is too lazy.

It must have been Hera then. Yes, yes, unless the sun has roasted my head down to the roots, that is what it was— "Hera was here!"

But why should she want me to go to the beach, divine lady? No matter which leader turns up, he will have no time for me there; they will be too busy saying hello to everyone—their families, the people. And then aside from the prize, I would have no business there myself, I having no son to welcome home or even a son-in-law, there being no daughter either. "Though I tried, Hera, if you are still around." And he had, filling his woman full of his juices time and time again through the years.

Never mind, why should I rush down there?

Soon it came to him—"Yes, that is it." There was going to be trouble, serious trouble, at Agamemnon's palace that night if the king appeared. For as everyone knew, the queen, Klytaimnestra, fine though she was with her white face and dark curls, had been living there while he was away with his cousin and archenemy, the prince Aigisthos. And even though she had made no children for the man and he would probably run away—is doing so now, I expect—someone is sure to unfold it all to the king, perhaps right away. The result of course will be that he will strangle her. And then he will be all for tracking that Aigisthos down, wherever he has gone to, to do the same to him.

"And then I will never—". . . .

His wife scrambled up when he came through the doorway and would have followed him. But—"No, woman, leave me be."

He ran past her toward the gate—"My bowl! My prize!" . . .

She gazed after him—let him go if he wants to. But no, I do not mean that. Only, if only he would—

Then when she saw that he did not return she stepped outside to peer down the road and realized that he would not, it was empty—"I must—" And she rushed into the house for the carafe and out again with it.

She was only going a little way to a hill, not after him— where is he off to anyway? To see them come in probably, the ships. But what was all that about a bowl? "Who knows? There is always something with him."

Soon she was there and, clearing away some brush from the mouth of a small cave, got down on her hands and knees and crawled into it and lay there for some moments face down, to spell herself.

Then she began to feel it coming on again, just as it had every day or so all the way back to her first bleeding-time, maybe even before that. It was like a grasping in there, except that of late sometimes it had been different; now, again. It was deeper; she could no longer get at it with—eh, anything.

Gradually the thing became worse, until it was like a clawing. And then she rolled over and her eyes sought the ledge above and the sandy yellow figurine that stood on it. Featureless it was, but it had pointed breasts and wide hips and outstretched arms, and that was good enough. "Oh Hera, can't you make him like before?"

She raised herself up on an elbow and tipping the carafe poured a few drops of the precious red on the ground. "At least once in a while?"

Then she took a little swallow herself. "Just once?"

.

In the watchtower of Mykenai paced one who though still in the king's service and thus helmeted and cuirassed and doing his turn up there was truly out of favor with Hera or something. For Agamemnon on sailing away—was it ten, yes, ten years ago—had left him behind. And every time he thought about it, which was every moment of every day almost—honestly it was enough to make him want to kick.

Why I served with his father, Atreus, before that start-up was born. And we went everywhere together, even to the coasts of Thrace. Either we traded there, or else if they proved unwilling, the natives, we—"Har!" Now that is what I call experience.

What made it worse, who had been chosen to go to Troy

instead but—"That's right"—his own son, a boy practically, who could not tell gold from bronze.

And the boy's only knowledge of a field was with that loose-legs, his wife!

Well (he leaned on his spear), soon it will be light out, and then the captain will be sending someone up here with something for me to eat, you never can tell, maybe a little of that good meat left over from last night.

Now there is a man after my own heart, the captain—

But what is this? Beacons! There were beacon fires everywhere.

And there were. First there had been one on Argos, then another on a nearer hill, then one closer yet, and now they were all around him as far as the eye could see.

"Must tell the captain!"—as he rushed almost sliding down the ladder. "Must, must, must!"—taking the stairs two-three at a time.

"Captain, sir!"—as he charged into the great hall. But there was no chance. Some serving girls who were on their knees with sponges gave a cry as soon as they saw him and ran out to the courtyard to see—eh, girls—and the captain, who had been standing talking with the stewardess on the other side of the hearth, began walking after them, she with him.

"You may go"—to him quietly on passing.

"Thank you, sir. Thank you."

Yes, a good man, the captain—as he clop-clopped down the staircase. And if that is Agamemnon's fleet coming, which I'm inclined to believe is so, too bad for him and the stewardess. For then it will have to be over between them—her husband is with it.

I suppose it is the end for the prince and the queen too. Yes, the captain is probably on his way to tell him right now, or he soon will be. And then he will leave, very likely go back to the temple, where he came from.

He waved to the guard at the gate, another old left-behind, then set off down the road. Who knows, there might be a good fight around here one of these days. If Agamemnon learns everything, which seems certain (the girl Elektra will tell him probably), he'll go and ask the priestess for Aigisthos, and if she agrees—well, it will be interesting.

An odd way that Aigisthos has of handling a throwing-spear. Uses it all wrong, to thrust with, but he's fast at it, and deadly, considering how small he is. Saw him finish off a nasty spitting mountain lion in that way once when he took me hunting with him; got it in the neck just one time, in-out, and that was that. Yes, it should be good.

And there will be another interesting fight around here, come to think of it, if he, that son of mine, does not bring home anything worthwhile from Troy. Why I will take him and the girl (his child) and his wife (were she not under the earth) even his mother (had she also not departed from this life) and kick all of them!

As he entered the town, from over the courtyard walls came sounds of women talking and laughing and of one singing alone. Now there, there is the real evil in this world, these women chattering and screeching all the time.

And worse—"Yes, worse"—taking advantage of their men while they were away and chasing after anyone happening along the road, even boys, and—

From somewhere a baby wailed. "There, you see"—the proof.

But never you fear, they will catch it now. Yes, now that their men are returning home, they will get it but good, with slaps and punches and maybe even—

"Kicks!"—sending a stone skipping with his foot.

Reaching his own gate, he marched through it and into the house. There he carefully stowed away his helmet—precious boar's tusks—in its wicker basket and slung the rest of his gear—tough leather—on a peg. Then taking up some bread that he had in a pouch and a waterskin and his spear once more, now as a walking stick—"We will soon see"—headed for the door again.

"Hey, old grandfather"—from somewhere near the hearth—"where are you off to?"

"The beach"—still moving.

The small head came up. "Is he here then? Is my father here?"

"It looks like"—as he went outside.

"Wait for me!"

But he kept on going—if she wants to come along, well, let her. . . .

She jumped up, grabbed for her tunic (one of his cast-offs cut down so that it fell only to her knees) and ran out of the house and down the road after him. Then, having caught up with him, she sort of skipped along by his side, feeling good in the mild warm sun.

I wonder what my father looks like? Truly try as she might, and she had many times, promising Hera all sorts of nice things, she could not remember. All that she did, and that seemed very shadowy, was to stand as a very small child together with her mother and grandmother watching a line of chariots pass along here and waving at one of them.

At least he will be strong and fit; yes, that much I can count on, I think, for men, especially warriors, normally are so. Only, Hera, make his arms sinewy; I like them that way. And see that he is not as—big as the captain, please.

What good times we will have, he and I, when he is back here again. So she had dreamed for ever so long, day and night; now she had begun doing it once more. For the next best thing to using real weapons against living breathing flesh herself, she had decided once, is to be a companion to someone who has, maybe even one day to—she pictured the two of them facing a wild boar together as it came charging wildly out of a thicket.

Now a panther has sprung hissing and snarling from a tree, and she has taken her wrist-dagger and driven it— "Aaah!"—right into its heart.

.

Grim was the captain's mood, bleak-black so, there where he stood in the courtyard with his woman beside him gazing out toward the sea, ringed round now with signal fires all spent—just wriggles of smoke like singed hairs.

For that was Agamemnon coming; of that he was certain, as Diomedes surely had suffered some mishap toward the end. Agamemnon had not appeared sooner because— well, with all the treasure there was to load he had made a late start, or else he had stopped off to do a little raiding after, or—there was some other reason.

But what does it matter why? It is he, that is all. And now I will lose her.

And it did not seem fair somehow, considering. For she and her husband had been married only several months at most when he left—whereas with her and me it has been much longer.

But fair, what is fair? Would it be fair for the husband not to get her back after serving the king all that time?

Still maybe it is for the best; yes, maybe I will be better off without her. Nor was this idea a new one. So he had told himself now and again during those years with an eye to this day.

After all she is no longer young. Indeed she was somewhat along the way even when we began. And her breasts had dropped a little more since then, and her flesh was less firm, especially around the midriff where he liked it to be.

Also she is, in fact has always been, very plain-looking. It is her hair, almost all grey now, together with those greyish tunics she wears that does it.

Why if the truth be known, in the beginning it was she who sought me out, not the other way around, as some people might suspect.

Of course I did go to her room that night. But then she invited me there. And so it had been. She had come down to the garrison house one morning (this was five or six days after Agamemnon's departure) and asked if he could stop by later to discuss something concerning her work in the palace. And he, seeing nothing unusual in this, what with her probably having much more to do and doubtless more than the ordinary number of problems to go along with it now that her husband and the other men from up there were gone, had agreed and in all good faith.

But I did make the first move. And that he had, suddenly in the middle of their conversation—he never knew why exactly. Was it the heat from her hearthfire or what?— taking hold of her and putting his mouth on hers.

Even so there it would have ended had she not—yes, she did—begun pushing against him, his thighs. For what with one thing and another he had lost his balance and fallen backwards onto the bed dragging her with him.

And the next he knew, their tunics were up around their waists and—

Of course it is altogether possible that she will be better off without me, it now struck him, this for the first time. For her husband, when he was home, served in the great hall, like her, as chief steward. So the worst he ever smelled of was a little spilled wine or slopped meat juice—which unfortunately is not the case with me, surrounded as I always seem to be with horses and dogs and things like that.

He probably treated her better too. I don't know what it is, but every time I get near her, it appears, I step on her foot or knock into her or something.

And what is worse yet, the worst, and for the life of me I cannot understand it, no matter how much I want to please her, almost as soon as my phallus is in her—and I even give it a good squeeze and sometimes a pinch beforehand—it is finished; it loses its juices.

She of course has never said anything to me about it, gentle woman that she is. And I, of course, have always done it to her again after a while and nicely then, pressing here-there the way she seems to like it, until she makes a big sigh, ah. Still it must be annoying to her. Didn't the corners of her mouth turn down the last time it happened—when was it, when did we do it last—two nights ago?

Yes, surely (shoulders, arms, limp) she is glad—what am I saying, overjoyed!—to have her husband back again. . . .

The stewardess in the meanwhile had been trying hard not to saw on her lip. Patience, only have some patience, it will soon be over. Yes, in a little while you will be rid of him and forever.

But to think of having done it with him all those years, him with that gritty neck of his and those coarse scratchy chest hairs.

Why he would never even let himself be sponged down, no less get into a tub, unless I threatened to have nothing more to do with him.

And everyone, all of my serving girls, knew about it, I am sure. They were laughing at me too.

And when I remember how I had to chase after him at first! Oh, the shame, the indignity of it. Imagine, staring at him every time we passed one another somewhere, and when that didn't have any effect (he seemed to look right through me) having to go down there to that place of his— so grimy—and, with all of his men standing around, practically beg him.

Well, soon, patience. For he, the one who used to preside over the roast in the great hall, seeing to it that each slice was carved exactly like the other and laid just so on the platter, soon those same fine hands of his will be all over me, stroking me gently, and his nice sweet thing curling into me.

He even flicks his tongue around a little down there, as I recall, which is more than I can say for this one, even though I have to do it to him sometimes, put that sour wrinkled thing in my mouth—to try to make it so he can do what he should have to begin with.

And that, I almost forgot about that! And after she had sworn only Hera knew how many times she would never— never forget. Oh, how she loathed him for it, to use her in that way, as if she were a—

Why one time (just recollecting it sent her into a rage all over again) he did not even get to— And the stuff went all over her tunic, a fine new white one that she had put on just for him.

To please him!

True, in the end he always made up for it, sometimes more than amply. Still. . . .

It was quiet all at once, her girls having gone away without her noticing it. They had fathers and brothers in the ships and that was enough to make anyone scurry off like that.

What will become of him after, I wonder?

Eh, he will return to his old ways most likely. One goes and gives the priestess a little something. She has a girl lead you to one of their rooms there, and then as soon as you have done it with that one, this perhaps without her having exchanged even so much as a word with you, she gets you up and shows you out to the gate.

It is sad when one begins to think about it; that is all he has known aside from me. . . .

"Someone should tell the queen and him"—he, finally.

"I will if you like"—she.

He considered for a moment. "No, I'll go."

"What will they do?"

"Do?"—his voice boomed out. "What is there to do? He must leave, that is all."

"Will he return to the temple, do you think?"

"Where else can he go?"—loud again.

And he moved away toward the stairs.

There is nowhere else—as he went up them. Nowhere—striding down the corridor.

He halted before their chamber. Then hearing no sound in there—they are still asleep in all likelihood—he knocked softly.

There was some movement. Then the doors parted a little. "Yes?" It was Aigisthos.

Dimly he made out that the man's eyes were unsteady, and he wore only a loincloth, which he had probably just slipped on. "Sir"—and he told him.

Aigisthos nodded—thanks—and the doors closed.

So now what?

He began to walk away.

But just then the doors came open again, this time almost flying, and there she was, Klytaimnestra, all bundled up in a robe, white, long-flowing, and her eyes, those dark eyes of hers, looked startled too, ah. "Captain, a chariot."

"Yes, my queen, at once."

Of course—he thought, going below again. And finding his woman still there in the courtyard—"As I said."

"Shall I see to his things?"—she.

"Hmm."

And he went on.

At the stable—"Get that chariot ready"—through the doors to the boy working there. Then he headed down the ramp for the bastion to watch Aigisthos go.

For they were friends in a way, had been almost since the moment they met. . . .

Oh, that day, that was some day. I will never forget it as long as I live.

He had gone up to the pine forest in the morning with only one thing in mind, to try to bring back a deer or something for his woman, the arrangement between them having been several months old by then. But he had gotten only a short distance from his chariot when he spied this stranger up ahead in some brush.

Naturally he had guessed who it was immediately, for the king had told him about the feud between the two families soon after taking him into his service a few years before. And since every able-bodied man in the country had gone with him to the war, the unknown one could have been no other. With the garrison reduced in strength as it was, this Aigisthos had apparently thought it safe enough to stray from the precincts of the temple and try his hand at a little hunting himself. He was on his haunches, fitting a string to a bow.

What a piece of luck, he had thought, and quickly sneaking up on him, kicked him over. Then finding him unwilling to put up a fight (although a knife and a throwing-spear were lying within his reach), he had dragged him to his feet and tying his wrists up good behind him—with his own bowstring, hah—spear-butted him back to the chariot, his idea having been to let the queen deal with the culprit down in the citadel.

But I should have known better; where was my head? For Klytaimnestra was in a bad way then, the king having recently sacrificed one of their daughters, as it happened her favorite child—so Hera would help him in the war, I suppose. And since her return a short while before from Aulis, where the ritual had taken place, all she had done every day was sit around and look gloomy. So she was in no condition to handle anything, let alone a matter as serious as this one.

But even if I had realized this and not brought him before her, what could I have done? Could I have killed him just like that, without a fight? Of course not, no more than he kill me—as I was soon to see.

Upon their arrival he had taken Aigisthos straight up to the great hall, this being where Klytaimnestra usually did her sitting and staring, and found her on this occasion (it was not always so) on the throne.

At first, on his having explained—"This is Aigisthos, your enemy"—she had made no response.

Had she heard him? Perhaps not. So he had repeated it. Only it was with the same result. Then he had tried once more, but still she had remained silent.

Finally, what to do now, he had thought. Should he send a few of his boys out to find the king, wherever he was— Aulis, Troy—and keep the man locked up somehow until then or what?

Just as he was on the point of going away again, however, she had begun to smile. "Enemy?" Then to laugh. "I have no enemies, at least—" And then she had grown solemn again. "Not here."

"My queen?"

"Set him free."

"But my queen— "

"You heard me."

"But—"

"Free!"

So having proceeded as he had, what could he have done then? What but take his dagger and cut his prisoner loose, which he did.

Then, thinking that the man would probably consider him, the chief servant here, as one and the same with the king, his enemy, he had gone out to the courtyard and waited around to see what would be.

A while later Aigisthos had joined him. "She wants me to stay"—he. "I suppose I will for a little"—with a grin and a shrug.

Oh Hera, I was never so— Even now thinking about it,
I—

What have we here? For now as he gained the top step of
the bastion, there before him was the same face as the
queen's, high forehead, small nose, full wide mouth—it was
the princess Elektra.

What is she doing here, this girl? She despises Aigisthos.
"My princess?"

"My father is coming."

"Yes, my princess, I know."

They stood for some moments facing Argos and the sea,
a rush of wind on their backs. Then feeling a certain
warmth like a hot hand on his neck, he turned to see the
sun rosy-wheeling into the sky. At the same time high
above in the watchtower, which was all radiant with the
new light, a dark figure appeared. "Your mother"—he
nodded.

"Yes."

So where is the man?—he shifted from one foot to the
other.

Soon, in another moment, there was a rumble, and the
next thing he knew the chariot was below him about to go
through the gate. Catching Aigisthos' eye, he raised an arm
—goodbye. Aigisthos did the same.

So, a good man—calling to mind, as the vehicle went
down the road, the many times they had hunted together
since that meeting of theirs, particularly yesterday, when
Aigisthos had been very keen at tracking for them.

Well, maybe I'll get to see him again sometime over at
the—

What's the matter with Elektra here? Her face was all
pinched up, and it looked as if she were going to bawl. "My
princess?"

"My father will see to him. He'll take care of you!"—to
the road, now empty.

"My princess."

But no, she wouldn't listen, indeed sprang away. And what was there to say to her anyway?

Too bad—his eyes following her, now at the bottom of the stairs as she headed toward the palace. I imagine that it wasn't pleasant for her here all these years with Aigisthos and her mother together like that and her father away.

Will she tell on them, I wonder?

I hope not.

For it will make the king terribly angry—with her mother, surely.

Us too perhaps, my woman and me.

.

Smooth, worn—soldiers' stairs—Klytaimnestra ascending. One foot after the other, so.

Then the ladder, swaying.

Be careful! Almost—

Still onward, up.

What a struggle it had been with Aigisthos. I am weary just thinking about it. For a while it seemed as if he would never go.

He had begun (this was just after she had spoken with the captain) by suggesting that they wait and see. "After all how do we know that it is your husband? It could be some other."

But she had suspected even then what he was about. How else could she have responded except as she had? "Who else could it be then—Diomedes?"

"Yes, among others."

"But he is just too long overdue," she had insisted. Yes, either the gulf had swallowed him up or else, and this was even more likely, he had taken his loot and slave girls and gone elsewhere.

"What about his wife?"

"He didn't care much for her, as I recall."

"Well then, maybe it is someone else—Menelaos or Odysseus."

"They have been away from home for a good long time too," she had reminded him. Surely they would want to go back there first—to Sparta, Ithaka—before paying a visit here.

"It could be another then."

"Who? And what would he want here, whoever he is?"

"I don't know, a stranger."

"There is none in my husband's world, only you"—with a sly look.

And then he had disclosed it, what was really on his mind—"Do you honestly expect me to leave you like this?"

At which a kind of blind heat had arisen in her. But knowing full well that she dared not let him see it, that is, if she hoped to win—"We agreed that you would"—she, as evenly as possible. (And they had many times, not only in recent months, expecting the fires at any moment, but also over the years, anticipating this one.)

"Yes, but now—"

"What is so different about now; it is the time, that is all."

"Yes, but it means that you will be—" And then he— "Why not come with me then?"—making her resign herself to considering the alternatives all over again.

"You know that is out of the question." As soon as Agamemnon learned, she had once more pointed out, which would probably be immediately on his landing, he'd go right after them and find them too no matter where they went. Nor would it be of any advantage for someone to take them in. As soon as he drew up all angry and armed with his men, their protector would lose no time in handing them over to him. "That goes for your priestess too, I'm afraid."

"What if we were to try somewhere far away?" Even if

they started out now, there was still time. They could make a run for it to Korinth—"There is always some ship or other there, I think"—and then go on to Sidon or Egypt or anywhere.

Yes, yes, she knew all that, but as she had explained before, the distance would make no difference. Agamemnon would still pursue and if he did not catch them they would spend the rest of their lives constantly fearing that he would.

At this he had begun to lose patience—"Don't be so sure about that." Now, having given everything some more thought, he had a new idea. Perhaps her husband, expecting a disagreeable reception from her because of the child, would be relieved to find her beyond his immediate reach— "Especially with a young captive princess by his side all eager to please."

That was a blow, a harsh one, and she had needed a little time to recover. It was not that she cared for Agamemnon, hardly. Probably she never had. But this had hurt, though why exactly she would have been at a loss to say.

Then she—supposing that they did go to one of those places and he did not come after them—"How shall we manage to make a life for ourselves there?" Even if they learned the language, their fair skins would always set them apart. Not only that, once their gold was gone (indeed— "How much can we find to take with us at the last moment like this anyway?"), the natives would have no mercy on them—"and we shall probably end as their slaves and doubtless be separated from each other as well."

Now his patience was completely at an end. "Never mind, I'll stay and fight! That is what I wanted to do in the first place, if you remember."

Upon which the blind hotness had returned, and it was even harder for her to contain than before. Still—"Helped by whom, the men of the temple? Surely the priestess would never allow it."

"The captain then."

"You can't be serious."

"Well, why not? He likes me, doesn't he?"

"The captain has been and always will remain loyal to my husband; make no mistake about it. That is the way he is, and neither you nor I or even she is capable of changing him in that respect."

"But you can never tell. At least let us try. Ask him!" For if the captain joined them, so too would the rest of the garrison, or a good part of it anyway, and—

A quiver had passed through her. "Please!"

True, it would be a handful of boys and old ones against regulars seasoned in the field—

"I beg of you!" She had begun to tremble.

Still if they were tired from their sea voyage, why he and the captain, they just might be able to—

"No!"—shaking in earnest.

And now seeing this, he had—no more—drawn her to him.

Then had come, at last, the end. Calm once again after a few moments, she had slipped out of his arms and stepped back to face him. Those eyes of his, she had said to herself, those good brown eyes always so sensible, let them be so now. "If I told you that I know how difficult it must be for you to go like this, would it make a difference?"

He had considered. Then softly—"Yes."

"All will be well, I promise you."

"But what if someone, Elektra, tells him before you have a—"

"Yes, she might; it is a risk. But it is a single one."

Again he had reflected. Then finally—"All right."

And then—ah, those eyes down—it had been her turn to comfort. . . .

Now there in the watchtower with the signal fires, all pale yellow twinkles, receding in the distance like falling stars, she began leaning to one side and rested a hand on the balustrade for support. Nor was she alone in this. Everything—the pine forest, all black-green, on the lower reaches of the mountain just beyond, the dusky countryside all around, even the grey-blue shadowed walls of the citadel directly below—seemed to have disposed itself for waiting too.

And soon there was something. She felt it on her back, warm, airy and light. He has returned then, my man, for there is another way, one that we had not thought of before. It came to him just like that as he was getting into the chariot. Imagine it, after all those years of trying. Yes, in another moment his arms will be sliding round me again and he'll be telling me about it, the new way. And then we will be silent for a time while my mind works to understand and accept it, and his to reassure itself that it is after all feasible. She half-turned.

But no, he was not there, nor anyone else either. Rather it was the sun, lying just below the dip between the pine forest mountain and the next one. The sky was a wildfire of reds and yellows there.

So he will be going after all. Let him then, for it is still the best way—

Even though I did not altogether convince him of it.

She looked down—at any moment now. There; he was rolling down the ramp and out onto the road. Her eyes followed his back as far as the bend. Then there was nothing, only dust settling. Is it so then? Is he really gone?

She considered how long it would take him to get through the town, then when the time seemed to be up, peered beyond it. But no, there was no more dust even, not so much as a wisp; only the land all pinkened now and here and there red and yellow flashes upon it.

So, it has happened, gone! Her hands came together and the fingers locked.

No, I must not—letting them fall to her sides again. Remember, this is how you wanted it to be.

And it was a good thing too that she checked herself then, for now there was someone nearby. Yes, this time a person is really here—she had heard a step as well as sensed a presence behind her.

Who is it, the captain? No, he was down on the bastion a moment ago. She looked—he still is. As for Elektra, she was with him then, so it is too soon for her to have climbed up here. Then, who? She turned slowly.

Ah, the stewardess, only the stewardess, only she.

But why is she here? Does she or the captain suspect something?

Know!

What am I thinking, of course not, of course they don't.

For you see—all of you—there is nothing. Yes, we have no plan at all, Aigisthos and I. And we left it that way on purpose—

Expecting that it would happen at the right moment, whenever that would be.

I don't even know what kind of weapon I will use, though chances are it will be a knife, as that is probably the easiest one for me to handle.

And when that moment comes, perhaps right there on the beach, yes, just as he has climbed down from the ship and his feet have touched the ground, and with everyone looking on—his men, the captain, she here now, even the children—I will take it, the knife, and without a word, no, no greeting, not even an accusation—nothing—

Plunge it into his chest!

But first, before that, for our child—mine!—and everything else that he has done—

Into his face—his eyes!

— *II* —

"Will you dress, my queen?"—the stewardess, now beside her.

Dress? "Dress?" She looked down at herself. "Oh." She was still in the robe that she had pulled on when the captain had knocked. "Yes, presently."

But how pale she is, the stewardess. Yes, her face seems even sallower than usual. Is something troubling her? But of course, her husband, the captain; today she will be getting the one back and will have to give up the other, and perhaps she would like it the other way around. For all I know, she might want to keep both of them.

"It must be soon, my queen, or we will be late."

"Late?"

"For the beach, my queen, the landing."

Ah, the landing. "I'll do it presently."

"But the captain, he—"

"I said I would do it. Presently!"

"Yes, my queen"—withdrawing.

Now hungrily almost her eyes sought the pine forest again, which along with everything else around her was considerably lighter, shadowy-green. Ah—she raised an arm as if to touch it. The coolness of it—bringing her hand to her face.

She and Aigisthos had been up there together yesterday. He had gone hunting with the captain, and she had waited and watched from the chariot. Then, there being no room for the three of them what with the catch of a fine stag, she and he had walked back down to the citadel, but not at once. First they had received some food and drink from an old shepherd they had come upon. Then further on, as shelter from the heat, they had found a cool secluded spot and stopped to rest for a while. And seeing pine boughs all around above them (it was like a roof overhead), she had ventured, "Wouldn't it be nice to stay here always?"

"No, not at all." Think of the cold and rain in winter, he had reminded her, to say nothing of mountain lions and wild boars and Hera only knew what else that might come to trouble them. And then as if these were not bad enough, there would be no stewardess to wait on them and growl.

They had laughed, but only with their mouths. In their hearts had remained a coldness—the end might be coming soon.

Then their voices died away, it had grown very still there, and turning to one another, they had—yes. . . .

He knew everything of course. She had told him one night (this was some days after the captain had found him, and they had already begun together). It had taken a long time, the telling, all through dinner and then some in her chamber in the chairs before the hearth.

·

Her father was Tyndareos, high-king of Sparta. There were three other children, her sister, Helen, who was a year older than she, and their younger brothers, the twins Kastor and Polydeukes. While she and Helen were still small, Tyndareos had adopted Penelope, an orphaned niece of his who was around their age, and had her brought up with them.

As far back as she could remember, no one had ever thought very much of her prospects. For besides being a younger daughter, she was as nothing compared to Helen in looks, Helen with that smile of hers, all sparkling black eyes and melting mouth, and her soft white skin and fine black hair too. Yes, Helen would marry well, everyone in the palace was always fond of declaring, the first-born of a high-king at least, if not then of a king, while she, Klytaimnestra, was destined for the second or third son of one such or, if through some mischance she were to lose such attractive features as she possessed, some offspring of a kinglet in the hinterlands somewhere. So that all in all the future held only slightly more promise for her than for cousin Penelope, whose looks (she had blue eyes and fair hair) to say nothing of her dowry were hardly worth speaking of.

"You can imagine my surprise then when—" But this was getting ahead of her story.

Several years after the onset of her bleeding-time Tyndareos announced that he was ready to marry the girls off and sent around proclamations to the various royal houses of Greece and one or two abroad also, so that their princes would come to them as suitors. Around the same time something extraordinary happened at the palace one night.

"As I recall"—it was drearily warm, and with dinner over Tyndareos was nodding on his throne (he was getting on in years), her mother and some of the older serving women were sitting and talking quietly among themselves, and they, the girls, were close by drooping over their embroidery. Only the boys, her brothers, were absent, being off somewhere or other on their horses, maybe using their fists; they were rather wild. Suddenly there was a commotion outside in the courtyard, and the next moment two young strangers came rushing in with a pack of guards at their heels, a few of whom seemed to have gotten the worst of it from them.

Tyndareos, jolted to attention by this, demanded to know who the pair were. Whereupon the taller and more angular of them stepped up and told him that he was Agamemnon, son of Atreus of Mykenai; the other was Menelaos, his younger brother. At this everyone became excited, for while the faces were unfamiliar, Atreus never having honored an invitation from Tyndareos or issued one to him, the names were not, Mykenai being the nearest kingdom to the east of them and for some time, with Atreus' reign, one of considerable wealth and power.

But why were they here, these almost-neighbors, Tyndareos wanted to know? And how did they come to look like that, for they were exceedingly dirty and ragged and maybe bleeding a little too. Agamemnon explained, haltingly at first, for he was winded. The garrison of their citadel was off on an expedition with Tydeus of Argos, a special friend of Atreus, and it seems that someone, they were not sure who—("That was my father and I," Aigisthos had interjected here. "Yes, I know.")—had taken it into his head to attack them in force, and what with both gates on fire and about to give way and not enough men to do anything about it Atreus had packed his two sons off to try to find help somewhere.

Tyndareos, being no fool, did not have to hear any more. Instantly he ordered up arms and men and chariots for them. Then before they galloped off, he made Agamemnon promise that when his trouble was over, he and Atreus and Menelaos too, of course, would come back as his guest-friends. And naturally everyone applauded such generosity toward the hapless princes. "I too, I must confess. My eye was on Menelaos."

Around a month or so later they returned. By then the palace was full of young men who had come in response to those notices of Tyndareos. So that when the captain of the guard informed him of the approach of their party, quite a crowd collected down at the gate to have a look. Upon which everyone, Tyndareos included, could hardly contain himself, for there was Agamemnon all in glinting gold and purple—helmet and mantle—standing tall in a magnificent golden chariot. Menelaos (who had on a plain white tunic) managing the reins seemed like a mere servant beside him.

Nor was this all. Agamemnon then told her father that Atreus was dead, he was the new high-king of Mykenai. And how everyone oh'd and ah'd at this, she along with them. How could one not be impressed?

"At the same time there was something about him—I don't know whether it was those high sharp cheekbones of his or pale thin lips or—I don't know. He made me feel uneasy. But perhaps I have added this in retrospect."

In the days that followed Agamemnon divided his time between her father's chamber, where they were frequently alone together for long periods, and his woods, hunting with Menelaos and sometimes one Palamedes of Nauplion, whose father had been a special friend of Atreus.

Soon another attached himself to them and went with them there, Odysseus, who came from Ithaka, a small island kingdom somewhere way in the west. This Odysseus, who was rather odd-shaped, being all chest and thighs, nevertheless possessed considerable skill at games—wrestling, bowmanship, and the like—and he never let a chance pass of demonstrating it. Apparently he was very good at storytelling too, for every night in the great hall over where the men sat his mouth was constantly in motion and everyone else, Agamemnon included, laughing.

Her great fear in those suspenseful days was that

Agamemnon would save Menelaos for someone with better prospects and she would be matched with the Ithakan. So when she learned (from one of the serving girls, a special friend of hers, who had it from the guard outside her father's chamber) that she herself was to marry Agamemnon, and Helen, Menelaos, and that Penelope was to go to Ithaka—"Why I was quite surprised but pleased too, indeed rather happy."

Helen, on hearing this, was naturally very upset and went at once to find her father. But Tyndareos, so the report went, while listening to her with sympathy, would not even consider a change in the plans, so eager was he for the connection with Mykenai. As to why Agamemnon had not chosen her to be his wife, his only explanation was "A man's taste is not always predictable, my child" or something like that. "Poor Helen. It was her first real disappointment or actually second. And with them coming as they did, one after the other like that and without any warning, she must have been, well, miserable. Who knows how much of what happened later on was owing to her state of mind then?"

Their mother and her friends, who almost worshipped Helen, were also distressed by this unexpected turn of events and since they could do nothing else about it, spread it around—"Half-believing it themselves, I suppose"—that Agamemnon had found their favorite a little too high-spirited for him. He was afraid, the young high-king, that she would make a fool out of him.

She herself as the day of the wedding approached was not without some reserve. Not because of this tale, which with its implications concerning herself she did not fully understand—"Did not until later. Now!"—but others that she heard about him and his father too. These were in circulation among the young men there and repeated to her by her friend the serving girl, and they were quite unpleasant.

According to one, Atreus had come into possession of Mykenai in a grossly unfair manner. That is, while a guest of the previous king, one Eurystheus, when the citadel was under attack by one Hyllos, a rival claimant to the throne, Atreus had deliberately delayed going to his aid, with the result that the invaders were driven out but Eurystheus perished. And what made it worse, Atreus was enjoying Eurystheus' protection at the time along with his brother Thyestes—("My father, yes"—Aigisthos)—both of them having been banished from their native Elis for killing another brother.

Worse yet was the story of what Atreus did to Thyestes on discovering that his brother had betrayed him with his wife, whatever that meant—"I still do not fully understand." He, so it went, slew Thyestes' sons (there were three of them) and then had their bodies dressed and cooked and served up to the father at dinner. Thyestes, it was said, had somehow managed to run away and take refuge in the local temple, and there he had remained— "Until the day of his attack on Mykenai with you, a new son."

There were whispers too about what happened to Thyestes on Agamemnon's arrival back at Mykenai with Tyndareos' men and his learning of Atreus' death. Surprising him on the throne—("They did not say where you were."—"I will tell you one day," Aigisthos answered.)— Agamemnon had dragged him out to the courtyard and thrown him over the rampart into the ravine below, then stood and listened rapturously to the roars and snarls of the wild beasts down there and the man's cries resounding over them.

"But unsettling as those tales were, how could I have

really taken them seriously? Remember how young I was and how confined my life had been until then. Such outrages were inconceivable to me. No, it was far easier to believe that they were the spiteful distortions if not outright inventions of their bearers, my husband-to-be's unsuccessful rivals."

And so they were married, the three girls, Tyndareos holding a fine feast for them. And what with all of the noise and bustle and she and Helen and Penelope too in new flounced skirts with their hair all floppy with curls and braids it was a happy occasion. Then toward dawn, after the men—husbands, father, brothers, guests—had poured the last libations to Hera and the other goddesses and gods, it was time to go, at least for her and Penelope and their husbands (the plan being for Helen and Menelaos to remain there in Sparta until Agamemnon obtained or built a citadel with a palace for them). Upon which everyone, including those two, trooped down to the gate to see them off.

"Oh how wonderful it seemed"—with herself in a dainty cart all festooned over with flowers and surrounded by a generous complement of Tyndareos' chariots, Agamemnon's resplendent one leading the way, and Penelope in a plainer cart with a smaller escort and Odysseus before them in an ordinary chariot. "But what a silly, unknowing, uncaring child I was then." . . .

"It is difficult for me to speak of this—you know. (And here she had turned away and he had made a movement toward her but changed his mind.) You see, so enamored was I of the idea of the wedding, that is, during those days immediately preceding it, that I did not give any thought to what would happen to me afterward. Oh yes, I would be high-queen of Mykenai and dwell in its splendid palace atop its sturdy citadel. But I never actually envisioned myself there in that setting with him, my husband and its lord.

As for *that*, I suppose that I knew as much about it as other girls of my age and station, Helen perhaps excepted. (I suspect that she sensed a little more in that way and consequently dared more.) I had looked at boys, that is, serving boys around the palace; who else was there? And alone in my chamber at night I had imagined, well, being with this one or that and his holding me round and kissing me. And feeling good about it in my body, I had—you know, as girls and boys will. But whether I ever linked this in my mind with what horses and dogs did for the sake of young when one brought a female and a male together, I am not sure; I rather doubt it. Or if I did, it was very vague in my mind and so of no real consequence.

One thing is for certain: I did not think of either of these, my private doings with myself or what I had witnessed in the stables and kennels, in connection with him, no, not at the time of the wedding or even then as I rolled through the mountains with his back tall and straight before me and moved ever closer to his home. Maybe considering what was to be it was just as well.

On our arrival here I, unaccustomed to being on the road like that (it took us nine or ten days at the least), was all wearied out, and a serving man, I remember, almost had to lift me out of the cart. Then two women helped me up the stairs and put me to bed, and I slept for I do not know how long. And then, after another came by with something for me to eat (the stewardess most likely), I slept again.

At length refreshed I opened my eyes and looked around. It was dark there in my chamber and, with the strangeness of everything, lonely. Before my departure I had asked my friend the serving girl to go along with me, but she had turned me down because of an attachment to a young man in my father's garrison. Now I was sorry that I had not tried someone else. And then not knowing whether it was dusk or early morning, nor was there any way of telling, the sky through the smoke-hole being a kind of greyish-violet, I felt even worse, as if—I don't know—as if I were dead but somehow still sentient. But perhaps I am exaggerating or else— and this is more likely—confusing my feelings then with what I was to experience somewhat later.

At any event it was sometime around then that the door opened and he came in, and without a word walked up to the bed, drew the covers back, and got on top of me. I felt a little pain somewhere down there, his hand there, but before I could fully grasp what was happening, there was a much worse pain, so bad that I could have screamed; probably I did. Then I felt him—you know. And then, the next moment, he was up and gone.

Some days later, when I had healed some (I had bled a lot, and it was very sore there for a while), the scene was repeated, and a few days after that again, and then again, and so on. Yes, that is how it began, that part of our life, and so it remained to the very end, the day he went off to the war.

How did I bear it all those years? Well, it was not as difficult as it might seem. The wanting was of easy solution, the easiest. I simply did as I had before. Though even this— Well, it was better than nothing, wasn't it?

The lack of closeness between us was more of a problem; all day long, mind you, he was either shut up in his archive room or away on one of his farms somewhere, so that except for those visits I saw him only at dinner in the great hall, if that. What with my earlier imaginings and having heard of or seen other couples, serving people and the like, behave otherwise with one another, I suppose that I expected something different there. But this too more or less ceased to trouble me after a while, especially with the coming of the children.

From time to time during those early years I had a little news about my family, this usually relayed to me by the stewardess from him, my husband. Among other things I heard that Helen had given birth to a little girl, Hermione (this was around the same time as my first, Iphigenia), and shortly after this that Penelope had borne a son, Telemachus. Then one day some years later, after Elektra or Orestes (I can't remember anymore), I learned of the death of Tyndareos. This was sad news indeed, for although I had always counted myself low in his eyes, favored at times, it seemed, even after his "poor, little niece," he was still my father. And I waited to hear more, curious as to how my brothers, now grown men but still rough-tempered, I expected, would divide up the kingdom's duties and wealth. But nothing further came, at least not at once. And then when something did—oh Hera.

It was just after the birth of Chrysothemis—yes, that is right—and as before I received it all from the mouth of the stewardess. It seems that Prince Paris of Troy, supposedly on a routine diplomatic visit to Sparta, had killed both of my brothers (under what circumstances I never learned) and made off with Helen and the contents of the treasury. Where was Menelaos at the time? Visiting old Nestor at Pylos. And why had he left his wife there in the palace with Paris about to turn up, Paris who had been among the suitors and whose smile was surpassed only by Helen's? She had my brothers to protect her, and then they appear never to have informed him of the impending arrival—why was anyone's guess.

A few days after the stewardess told me of this, Menelaos showed up, his face (round it was like a baby's) all full of distress, and soon afterward, the next day, I think, Odysseus came, also looking very concerned. And on their talking it over with my husband, it was not long before the two of them together with their friend Palamedes were off to Troy to try to persuade Priam, the king there, to get Paris, one of his sons, to give Helen back.

But this was not to be. In about a month or so the three of them returned by themselves. Apparently (it was an odd story) Priam, who was most cordial to them, offered to hand over the gold that Paris had taken, but as for Helen she was not in the city. Where was she? Off with the young man somewhere, but where he did not know exactly; at least that is what he said.

So the next thing one knew, Menelaos and Odysseus and Palamedes were rushing home to call up their men, and my husband was sending the news around to all of the kings of Greece and asking them to join him; they were going over to Troy to teach that Paris and his family a thing or two.

And I? How did I feel about this idea? Why I was wholeheartedly in favor of it, for regardless of what Helen and I may or may not have been to one another, as with my father I was still of one flesh with her. I even thought, and I am sure that I said it and more than once then, that if it turned out from her account that Paris had used some kind of treachery in killing my brothers, he or his father ought to be made to pay something for them.

Now, however, looking back on everything, I cannot help wondering. Is it possible that all of it, the killings, the abductions, and so on, has been misrepresented? That is, could my husband have been their real originator, of course with Menelaos' knowledge and help and perhaps Odysseus' too?

It would not have been easy to manage, having Menelaos go off like that, as if he did not know that Paris and his party were arriving, and making the embassies to Troy seem sincere. (There was another one later from Aulis, but with Diomedes as the third man instead of Palamedes. My husband had Palamedes tried and executed for something over there, I don't recall what.) Still wouldn't all that trouble have been worth it to him if in the end there was something to show for it, something like the gold of Troy, to say nothing of a ready-made kingdom—Sparta—for a younger and perhaps potentially troublesome brother.

At any event it seems inconceivable to me that he together with all those kings and their men went all that way to fight so hard just for the sake of getting a woman back, even one like Helen, or because of a man's injured pride over one's loss in that way.

Who knows, he may even have hatched the plan way back there in my father's woods. In that case the matches, the marriages—everything was false.

And if he did, then I am— The children too, we are— Well, what does it matter? It is over and done with. (And here her chin having sunk to her breast, he would have folded her to him. But no, not yet—she had moved away.) There is more; I haven't told you *everything* yet.

I cared very much for the children, perhaps too much, you understand. And of the four of them I was fondest of Iphigenia, the eldest. At first this was because she represented a change in my situation. For yes, now that I recollect it, as was not the case with the others, I cherished her and very deeply even before she was born, indeed almost with the first feeling of fullness in my breasts. But then with her coming I had another reason (and this too was almost instantaneous, soon after the midwife laid the tiny body on them), and it was confirmed in my mind as time went on— that with that very fair skin of hers and those very dark eyes and her hair so flossy black she would grow up to be more than fine-looking. Why, I became fond of dreaming, she might one day even rival Helen in that respect.

On my husband's sailing away, I looked forward to a pleasant interlude with her, when with him not there I could do more things with her. She could stay with me in my chamber at night, for instance. Imagine my surprise and distress then when a month or so after he was gone, Odysseus turned up here with a message from him that Iphigenia was to leave at once for Aulis (where he and his men had met the other Greek contingents) and be married to one Achilleus of Thessaly, a young prince who would become a powerful high-king one day.

"But she is so young," I protested. And it was so, she having only recently experienced her first bleeding-time. "Besides, what is the point of her marrying a soldier who will be in the field all the time. Why not ask my husband to wait a little, at least until the war is over?"

Odysseus, however, only shrugged and responded, "It is their wish."

I turned to Iphigenia, who was by me at the time— "Well, would you like to marry?" (Unlike me at her age she knew everything; I had made certain of that.)

She moved closer to me and leaned her cheek on my arm.

"There, you see," I said to him. "She is too young."

Odysseus nevertheless insisted that she go; I suppose he had no choice. As for me, he would take me along if I wished and I could discuss the matter directly with my husband and perhaps even the young man. I yielded of course; what else could I do?

It was an unpleasant trip, as one under such circumstances is bound to be, and Odysseus, who remained solemn in his bronze throughout it (a far cry from the carefree suitor I remembered), did not help matters any. Further, as we went along, I began to have misgivings about my ability to dissuade my husband. You must realize that I had never before discussed anything with him, let alone a matter as critical as this one; and it was apparently so to him as well as me.

Would I lose her then, my precious Iphigenia? It seemed so. But what a pity that it is to be so soon, I thought. For in my eyes she was no longer a child but not yet a woman. How nice if I could enjoy her as she was for a few more years, then dress her up in a flounced skirt, turn her hair into curls and braids, show her how to heighten the colors of her face, and send her on her way.

Yes, a pity, and it was all the more so when I recalled how little attention he had paid to her until then. The other children the same, that is, except for Orestes, whom he had taken up to the pine forest every now and then and to whom he had given a present or two.

On our reaching the camp, it was night, and we found him in his hut already stretched out on his pallet. Even so and fatigued as I was myself, almost exhausted, I decided to broach the subject then, lest it be too late in the morning.

But it already was, he told me. He had given his word to the prince.

"But the girl is too young! Can't you see that?" I argued. "And where will she go afterward? All the way to Thessaly? Alone?"

To this there was no answer, and he knew it; so he turned away as if to go to sleep.

Iphigenia came to me. "It is all right, my mother." And she kissed me. But no, it was not—not all right. He was determined to separate me from her, this creature whom I cared for more than anything else in the world, and there was nothing that I could do about it.

Now for the first time I felt truly bitter against him. And all that night I lay awake thinking about how unfair it was. Then finally I slept; and when I did, it proved to be her undoing and mine as well.

On opening my eyes (the sun was fairly high by then), I found myself alone. He was not there, the child either.

Gone! I jumped up and ran to the door and looked out. There were the ships drawn up along the beach, but that was all. Everyone was gone!

I whirled round and round, peering, straining. Where were they? What had happened to them all?

Then sensing or perhaps hearing something, I ran up a nearby hill that was covered with pines, and soon I came upon them, all of the men. And shouldering my way through them, at length I reached a clearing and recognized Menelaos and Odysseus and the other leaders around its edge. In the center was my child, kneeling at an altar; my husband stood on one side of her, a diviner on the other. Someone had torn her tunic open down to the waist, I noticed with alarm, and tearfully she was trying to hide with her arms what the hanging hair did not.

I was beginning to wonder at the ceremony—how strange it was—when suddenly something, a glitter, caught my eye. The diviner had just handed my husband a knife, and he had put it to her throat!

"No!" I screamed. And rushed toward them.

But someone knocked me down, Odysseus, I think, and the next thing I knew, I was lying in a cart, and my husband, still with that golden thing in his hand, was barking at a soldier holding the reins—"Get her out of here!"

The cart plunged forward. From behind there where they were someone shouted, I heard it—"To the gods!" And the whole place roared in response—"To the gods!"

.

"My child!" And oh, the pain! For now as she stood in the watchtower there came to her what never had before seemingly, an odd smarting under the ribs.

"Tired." That's what it is—realizing that her eyes were bleary too. And with good reason; it had been a long day yesterday. For having risen very early in order to trail along with Aigisthos and the captain, she had not returned here until nearly dusk, and then with venison for dinner—a treat—they had lingered late there in the great hall. Not only that, on the captain's coming to the door this morning, they had both still been dozing, so that while her man had gone to answer, she had begun frantically searching for something to slip on and try as she might failing to (though the robe was there all the time on its peg where she had hung it).

Do I dare go and lie down again for a while, maybe sleep some more?

Why not?

But what about the captain?

"Let him wait." After all if the ships are way down in the gulf, which is probably the case, it will be quite a while before they even enter the bay. So what's the rush? (As it is, the man always seems to be in a hurry when others are not.) So let him, in fact let them all, the stewardess, Elektra—"Everyone wait."

For sometimes when you are not quite right, I have found (beginning toward the ladder), yes, sometimes then a little sleep is just the thing.

.

"*Crik-crak*"—Aigisthos on his way. Of course my friend would have to give me the oldest chariot in the place.

What am I saying? It is beyond that stage; it was already in the shed waiting to be chopped up into firewood.

Except that—"*crik-crak*"—a fire would not have accepted it without a groan, hah.

Well, I probably would have done the same to him had I been in his position.

Still—"*crik-crak*"—will I make it?

Yes—remembering: he had asked the same question on that fateful day of his arrival here. In fact he had wondered as much twice that day, first after being caught with that useless stringless bow in his hands while lying where he had been knocked over and looking for some chance to get back at his assailant, obviously from the citadel, then later expecting he did not know what from her, Agamemnon's queen, so odd had she seemed there on the throne with her eyes half-closed and head leaning to one side. (This he had noticed between keeping his own eyes fixed now on the gilt royal griffins on the wall above her, now on the golden warrior statue by her side.)

Imagine my surprise then when she said that I could go if I wished and wouldn't I care to stay on there for a while and my further surprise—no, shock—when I, suspecting that this invitation might be the start of some game between those two, went out to find him, her captain, all pale in the cheeks at the sight of me. Why—recalling how up in the pine forest yesterday the man's spear had flown clean through the stag's shoulder—he could have flattened me easily, then in the courtyard or at any time thereafter. Well —"*crik-crak*"—maybe this is the blow, hah. . . .

He was entering the town now, and ahead on the road he found people on the move, women and girls mostly and on foot, but some also in carts with donkeys and mules and horses. They all seemed to have red and blue and yellow tunics on, and there were flowers, white, pink, and purple, in their hair, and here and there he noted strings of them like that around their necks too. A holiday, it's a holiday!

There had been a similar scene here the morning when they had all left, their men. How did he know? Why he was here. Yes, everyone at the temple, especially the young men, having talked of nothing else for a month, he had sneaked up here to the road very early that day and hidden himself in some brush beside it.

But he had not come to see the crowd, in fact after a while had grown somewhat impatient with how they had behaved, constantly milling around in the way and only shifting a little when a column of soldiers had to go by. Nor was he particularly interested in the latter, smart though they were in their new leather helmets and cuirasses with their small round shields slung over their shoulders and ration pouches swinging from their spears. No, all that he had wanted to get a look at was him, the high-leader. And eventually, everyone having backed way up, indeed some almost to where he was crouching, and hushed a little, he had gotten his wish. A chariot all of gold had come rolling along, and noting one standing alone within it in a boar's tusk helmet and bronze cuirass, he had heard them all confirm his suspicion—"Hail, Agamemnon!"

Only for a moment that view of him had lasted. Then he was gone with the garrison all a clatter of hooves and rumble of wheels behind him. Still he had not been regretful about coming. That having been the first time he had ever gazed upon this enemy of his, at long last he had learned what the man looked like: he had eyes like slits and a small mouth. . . .

Now at the turn-off with its row on row of olive trees on either side, he swung the chariot onto it—"*crik-crak.*" During the years when he was at the temple alone, that is, after his father was no more, this spot where the roads met had figured in a dream of his, a waking one. He used to imagine himself galloping off on one of the priestess' horses one morning with spear in hand and finding him there, Agamemnon, indeed just as he was finally to see him, all resplendent in his war gear; upon which, urging the horse on toward him, he had caught the fiend just so, with his spearpoint right between the chinstrap and cuirass-top.

I suppose that if I do not hear from her, my woman, by the end of today, I will be rehearsing that daydream again. Yes, in that case it will be as before, there will be nothing else.

For the truth was that his need was as pressing as hers. . . .

She knew everything of course; he had unfolded it to her, the whole story, over dinner one night some days after she had told him hers.

With it still fresh in mind, he had fallen to musing on the fresco facing them across the hearth. This showed how Atreus had become high-king there, that is, how the citadel had been attacked and its gates set fire to and battered in by Prince Hyllos, then how Atreus had saved the situation, though belatedly so as far as the king, Eurystheus, was concerned. Realizing that the artist's intention naturally had been to glorify Atreus, he being depicted small in the scenes with Hyllos and large, indeed larger than them all, with the crown on his head in the end, he could not help remarking that what she had heard about the matter was true—"Only they who did the telling did not know it all, and these"— the panels—"surely do not have it right."

For yes, Atreus did deliberately delay coming to Eurystheus' aid, but not so Thyestes. "I do not know the details, nor are they of consequence except for this": when the trouble was over, people hereabouts, mindful of Thyestes' gesture, called for him to become their leader.

"Why didn't he?"

"It's hard to say. He was weak, I imagine." He allowed Atreus to persuade him to let him reign in his stead, and in exchange for this Atreus said that he could do as he pleased here at the citadel.

"You mean lead the ideal life of the younger brother"— she.

"I guess."

"And the other story about Atreus, how after killing Thyestes' sons, he had their bodies cooked and served up to him at dinner, is that true too?"

"I don't know; I rather doubt it. But he did lead Thyestes and everyone else too to believe that he had, which more or less amounts to the same thing, doesn't it?"

Having settled everything to his satisfaction, Atreus began going off on those expeditions of his—"You must have heard about them." So with Thyestes left to himself here for long periods of time—"His wife, the mother of my half-brothers, was killed during the siege"—what happened was almost inevitable: he and Atreus' Aerope fell into one another's arms. Naturally when Atreus found out about it, which he had to eventually—"He reacted as anyone would under such circumstances, I suppose."

Unexpectedly returning home one day, he immediately had everyone summoned to the great hall for a banquet. And Thyestes, suspecting nothing despite the unusualness of the hour (it was noon) and haste with which the invitation had been issued, went. Nor did it especially alarm him that Aerope and his boys were not present and the meal was beginning without them; little Agamemnon and Menelaos had not come in yet either.

A serving man set a platter of unfamiliar meat before him, and wondering what it could be, he was just about to have a taste and see when he raised his eyes for some reason. There was Atreus looking at him and smiling—oddly.

Sensing that something was wrong, though what he had no idea—still, wrong—he jumped up and ran with all of his might, managing to get down the stairs, out the gate, and away.

Sometime later, while hurrying along a deserted road somewhere, he remembered the strange meat and that Aerope and his sons never had appeared for the meal. And then he knew or thought he did and fell—and knew no more.

"And after that? What became of him then?"—she.

"He was not sure. He recalled, he told me, being passed one day by some soldiers in a cart and that they burst out laughing on seeing him" (probably because of the way he looked; he must have been wandering around for a considerable length of time). Then later, but just how long after that he was at a loss to say, he found himself in a hut within the temple walls being ministered to by a girl there. And sometime after that this girl brought him an infant—"Myself"—which she said that she had made with him.

"And is she still there, your mother?"

"As far as I know. But I wonder if I would recognize her anymore. You see, she was a servant in the temple, and as I grew older, she spent more and more of her time in there and less of it with us . . . She had light-brown hair and greenish eyes"—with a smile that was not.

And here her hand, Klytaimnestra's, had found his arm, which had made him feel a little uneasy, such a gesture having been new to him then. Even so he had gone on with the rest of his account.

·

As far back as I can remember, my father had only one thought in mind for the future, to avenge himself on Atreus and regain the kingdom—or that is how it seemed. Toward this end and sometime during my childhood he quietly began gathering round him men who had or thought they had some quarrel with the king; one can always find a few of such anywhere, yes? Wisely, I think, he concentrated his search on the outlying areas and avoided the towns.

The time for action came some years later, during my youth. My father, if you remember, chose it well; Atreus was short-handed in the citadel that month. Also that particular night was a moonless one, and it was rather cloudy.

While he and some of our men (there were a dozen or so altogether) set fire to the main gate, I did the same to the rear one with the rest. And so much noise did we make in the process that Atreus must have thought that he was being attacked in force. On our staving in the charred timbers, we found that he and his had retreated up into the palace.

This we soon gained entrance to in the same way and came face to face with them, the defenders, in the courtyard. My father, somehow managing to get through to Atreus, struck him down with a single blow of his sword, killing him instantly, I think. Then Atreus' men, seeing this, put down their own; and there it should have ended. But no, my father fell on the body and began clawing at it, shouting the while, "No, not yet! You must not die yet! I have not finished with you yet!"

At this I tried to pull him away, telling him that it was all over, his enemy was no more. But so enraged was he that either he did not hear me or care to. So then frightened because I had never seen him like this before, this one person in the world I cared for, and worried too about what our followers might be thinking, I jumped on him from behind. But this apparently only angered him the more, and he threw me off and with such force that, my head having hit something, the next thing I knew my eyelids were stinging from the sun on them and I found myself alone.

I discovered him here by himself in the great hall; he was on the throne, just sitting there. But on my going up to him, he appeared not to see me, and when I shook him—"My father?"—he did not respond or even look at me.

I located the pantry and brought out some wood, and lighted a fire and some lamps, and went to him again with a little bread and wine. But he still did not move; he did not even refuse them.

I returned to the courtyard, not certain what to think. What was the matter with him? And more important what should I do?

I did not know.

While standing there thus, trying to come to some conclusion or make a decision, I noticed that Atreus' body was beginning to turn putrid, it having grown quite warm out, hot in fact. So I dragged it inside to the pantry. Then I went back out there and again fell to considering what to do. Agamemnon and Menelaos, who, I rightly guessed, had not taken part in the fighting the night before, would no doubt be showing up with help before long. Obviously with our men gone, my father and I had to leave here and return to the temple as soon as possible. But how was I going to manage this with him as he was, even slowly?

I went in again, praying for some change. But no, there was none—that is, except for a wetness, his water, running down his legs onto the floor. I settled down nearby him to wait, going over to shake him every now and then in the hope that something would happen. And there I remained all through that day and the next one and I don't remember how many after that, but in vain.

When it eventually became apparent that it was no use trying to rouse him, I thought of finding a chariot or cart below in the stable and hitching a horse to it and trying to get him to his feet somehow. I would support him down there with my shoulders, arms. But I could not do it; I simply could not. I was just not strong enough.

Still I did not give up. If I had been able to drag Atreus' body, I reasoned, why could I not do the same with him. But no, this attempt was futile too; tug as I might, I could not even get him to slide out of the seat.

And so, spying puffs of dust on the horizon from the courtyard one day soon after this, I left—by myself—waiting and still trying to think of some way to take him along to the very last moment. Agamemnon and his party were entering the front gate as I slipped out through the rear one.

.

"And the way your father died, is that story true too, the one I heard?"

"I guess so; I heard it too at the temple. I never thought that Agamemnon would—" His throat had gone dry. . . .

And now—"I have as much cause as you! As much cause!"—he, to the empty air with tears in his voice again. And I have a good mind to go back there to the citadel and tell her so, yes, even though she knows it, tell it to her

again, and do what I really wanted to do, still do, even if it
means my death and hers too, which probably it would.
Only—only—

Bells! There were bells jingling. Yes (he listened closely),
somewhere beyond the bend up ahead. That will be the
priestesses on their way to the beach. He drew the chariot
off to the side to wait.

Soon—

> *Hail to Hera*
> *Aie, Aie, Aie*
>
> *Mother of milk breasts*
> *Daughter of open thighs*
>
> *Aie, Aie, Aie*
> *Aie, Aie, Aie*

And there indeed they were, the yellow cart flanked by a
line of yellow-clad temple girls on either side, their bare
breasts bobbing and flounces swirling as they went, and in
it the three holy ones—elder, younger, and youngest—
black-haired and white-skinned of course and arrayed as
usual in black and gold, their jackets likewise parted at the
front and revealing flesh. Managing the reins was an un-
smiling youth in a loincloth, one of theirs naturally, and
attached to the rear of the cart by a yellow thong and stepping smartly along there, a pure white, gilt-horned heifer.

"So, Aigisthos, you are returning to us"—the elder, her
severely black-lined eyes and eyebrows and very red lips
making a perfect smile for him; the other two joined her.

"Yes, Hera." He knew her, of course, and the middle one
too, though when he last saw them, the elder was the middle one and the other the little girl. Also he and the elder
had played together as children, and in his youth she

among others had taught him, belly slow-rolling, thighs flexing, "how to use his phallus in a woman so she would welcome him back." Indeed it was she, he believed, who had once shown him a dark-haired baby girl that "they had made together," though what became of the infant after that he never knew. Ah, the temple.

"And your woman? What is she going to do?"

"She will remain where she is."

"I see. It is for the best, yes?"

"Yes, Hera."

"Will the king make trouble for us, do you think?"

"I don't know—"

"Well, we shall see. In the meantime range where you will, Aigisthos. Feel free."

"Thank you, Hera."

They gave him another smile and rolled on.

> *Zeus will come soon*
> *Help him plunge it*
>
> *Aie, Aie, Aie*
> *Aie, Aie, Aie*

He brought the chariot back onto the road and moved on himself, almost happy now. For this was home; he had almost forgotten it. He was going home.

Soon, having rounded the bend from which the procession had emerged, he heard sounds of water splashing and shouting laughter, and beyond the next bend the stream—Chaos, they called it—came into view, and there on the other side of it (you had to go across a shaky wooden bridge to get there) was the temple's outer wall, old grey-stone, with only Hera knew how many pairs of gilt cow-horns by now above the gate. Sunny-brown boys were swimming in the water and basking on either bank or else grappling with one another, free-for-alling it. So he had been once—picturing himself here as one of them.

Just as he reached the bridge, something beyond it caught his eye. Two girls in the short tunic of the novice were hiding in a little thicket over there, he made out, and he stopped to watch, expecting more or less what would be. Sure enough, all at once they sprang up and flew down to one of the older boys, who was perhaps asleep, and yanked him to his feet. "No, let me be!" he cried. "No, I'm too young!" But to no avail; they began dragging him toward the gate.

He gave the horse a tap with the reins and passed through it behind them, not without a smile, remembering his own experience like that. He had been smaller than this one at the time, but old enough, his novices had insisted, once they had gotten him into the temple there within and to their chamber. And they would not let him go, oh no, not until he was a good boy and had done it for them at least once. Then they had slipped off their tunics, and while one of them had held him down (though since he knew that he had to go through with it sooner or later there was no need; he was resigned to it, in fact now that it was really happening a little eager for it), the other had fallen to kneading his phallus.

And oh Hera, soon how big it had grown; he could hardly believe it. Why it had never gotten like that before, when he had done it to himself or with one of his friends! The girls had noticed it too. "Look, look what a Zeus he is!"—giggling. Then the one with the magical hands had drawn him onto her and—ah—pressed it into her.

But then almost at once his juices had come out, and how worried he had been. He was afraid that it was wrong and she would punish him, that one. But no, "It is expected," she had assured him. Then the other had made it big again—using her mouth; and then he less anxious but as willing, they had begun taking turns with him, each working his hips to suit herself, until at length, the three of them happy and weary, they had fallen asleep. . . .

The two persistent girls and reluctant boy had disappeared inside, and it was silent in the courtyard. He brought the horse to a halt under one of the fig trees. Then taking a pouch and skin from his pile of gear (for which he had the stewardess to thank no doubt), he hopped down and planted himself on the ground with his back against the trunk.

She likes me, the pale woman—reaching into the pouch and bringing out a hunk of meat.

Yes, even though she always looks at me so severely—biting off a piece and chewing it.

As why shouldn't she—nibbling on another, then holding his head back and squirting some wine into his mouth.

After all what have I ever done to her or her captain except wish them well—more nibbling and squirting.

Soon a little drowsy he slid down and closed his eyes and turned his thoughts to whom else—his woman, Klytaimnestra.

By standards here, he well knew, she was no more than ordinary looking, indeed with her fleshy mouth and large eyes perhaps not even that. In fact this morning, when they were talking things over, she had seemed (only now he realized it) more unpriestess-like than ever. Her mouth at one point, while telling him that he was the only stranger in her husband's world, had twisted rather than curled into a smile, and her eyes had become like fire-charred stones when he said (it wasn't very nice) that now that her husband had a young captive princess he would be glad to see her gone. Yet her imperfection was what he liked most about her (that is, so far as features were concerned), and this he had begun to do almost the moment that he had set eyes on her. Indeed from that time on they had never

ceased making him hunger for her (as one's tongue and
teeth do for meat sometimes), which he had never felt
about anyone here however extraordinary.

As for her, no doubt about it, she felt the same about
him, though at first, their first time together—well. Later,
when they had come to know one another better, she had
explained. "I was afraid that you would hurt me. And then
I had a feeling that my husband would somehow find out
and come flying back here and do I didn't know what to
me, yes, that very night." Still that time—that was some
time.

That same fateful day of his arrival, when he had informed the captain that he would stay on, the man had
gotten some woman, the stewardess in all likelihood, to
lead him to a room and bring him something to eat. But
still suspecting that there was some game between him and
Agamemnon's queen on his account, he had sat, then sort
of lain there for a while wondering if he should not return
to the temple after all; at least one always knew what was
what there. Then all at once (it was nighttime by then) the
door had opened, and she was there, Klytaimnestra.

"I suppose that you are surprised to see me here"—she,
with gravity.

He did not say anything or make even the slightest movement, afraid that the horrible game might be starting then.
But when nothing had happened after a little and she had
continued standing there in the doorway—she must be here
for me, he had decided. And why not, why shouldn't we, if
that is what she would like and it will make me happy too?
And with that he had gone over and drawn her to him and
touched her mouth with his.

Only, what an odd one: she had not shown the least
interest, indeed had just remained as she was, motionless
with her arms down at her sides. Still she had made no
objection, he had noted, and so he had stooped over and

nudged aside her robe (which like the one that she had donned this morning was open at the front and tied round with a little gold sash) and touched her breasts with his lips.

But this did not have any effect on her either, and for a while there he had been at a loss as to whether to proceed. All the same he had, having led her to the bed and made her settle back there, then stolen all the way down her body with his mouth and put it within the hairs, on the lip of flesh there. And that had done it.

But how strange. When soon he had crept up so that he was mouth-on-mouth with her again and his phallus was in her (she had let him), he had found her—why she was like fiery milk in there!

Imagine it, she had wanted me all along. . . .

But now thinking about it, how she truly had need of him in that way—and him alone—which after they had been together like that a few more times, it had turned out was so, he realized that he valued it as much that she cared for him too. For so she did and also exclusively—remembering how only a while ago her lips, soft and cool, had sought to comfort.

Why with the one and the other, her wanting and liking him—even though her way probably will not work and most likely nothing can and it is the end for us, and maybe I should have insisted on staying back there at least to defend her, it is enough to make one do anything to please her—

Even sit here under this tree so and wait everything out.

— III —

A yawn. A stretch. A sigh.

Time to get up. And where is he, Aigisthos?—Klytaimnestra, sliding her hand across the bed.

When first they went to sleep, it was always with his holding her round and her head resting in that spongy hollow between his shoulders and chest. Then later, with the end of that sweet slumber, came rolling away, she to lie on a side with an arm out, he something like that. But then, just as the birds began to call, "Wake up! The sun is coming!" she would seek him again, sometimes drawing a leg over his hips, which by his slightly stirring against her breast she knew that he welcomed.

I will find him in a moment—still touching round.

But at length she did not—so he must have gone off again. For sometimes he did that, stole away in the half-light to meet the captain down by the stable.

Then his warm spot is here somewhere—beginning to search again.

But no, in the end her hand discovered not even that. Nor was there a crease on the pillow either, and it was solitarily cool there too.

So, then? She opened her eyes.

But gone!—half-bolting up on remembering herself in the watchtower before and gazing at the dust rising from the road. And this is the day. The day.

Have I slept long? Is it late?—consulting the crack of sky above the hearth.

Of course not—judging from its light blueness. Besides, if too much time had passed, the stewardess would have come for me; the captain would have made her do it and in a hurry.

She settled back and shut her eyes again—just for a while longer. But now there was a knock at the door. "My queen?"

So there she is now, aware once more. "Yes?"

The stewardess entered with a tray. "Something for your strength, my queen. It will be a long day."

"Fine"—sitting all the way up. "Just fine"—taking it from her.

How really good it is of her to think of me in this way. And this was not the first time either, she recalled. At every painful or crucial juncture of her life, it seemed—after the birth of each of the children, on her return from Aulis—there the woman was with a little something for one's strength, and always as now the wedge of cheese and loaflet were arranged prettily and the gold of the goblet shone so.

"Shall I see to your bath now, my queen?"

"Hmm"—moistening a piece of bread in the wine.

The woman withdrew.

Ah—sucking on it after having slipped the good red morsel into her mouth.

Soon distantly she heard water tapping on metal, which somehow brought her man to mind again.

Last night—

·

Little red tongues are going on the hearth, licking there, and she and he are lounging by it, talking quietly, waiting.

Soon she comes, the stewardess, a girl with her, and they bring slivers of roast meat all dusted over with thyme and rare piquant artichoke hearts and fleshy black olives and a crispy wheaten loaf.

"This looks very tasty"—he to her as she serves them. "I hope that you have saved something for yourself—and others."

The woman gives a little nod, flushing, and mixes and pours their wine and hurries away.

They burst out laughing.

Still—"One should not tease her so."

"Yes, I suppose"—he.

And they continue eating in silence.

Then finished, they take each other's hand and turn toward the fire again and think back to the morning. How fresh it was up in the pine forest at first. But then later—

Now the grey woman is there again, this time with a bowl of hard cheeky pomegranates and sweet yellow pears, ebony figs and grapes, cool green, thin as fingers.

Where has she found all of it like this, so early in the season? For clearly these are the first fruits of somewhere, but where?

Well, they're here now.

His eyes are glowing with it. The gold of the bowl—

·

The sound of water on metal had ceased. Now at the door—"It is ready, my queen."

"Coming"—quickly consuming the rest of the little meal and draining the goblet.

Then she rose, and they went down the corridor to the bath. There the woman gathered her hair back, pinned it up and helped her off with her robe.

It seems strange being all alone here with this one and

not having any silly-giggly girls around to run and fetch things, like more wine. She stepped up and into the tub, the woman lending a supporting arm—"I need a sponge."

"Here we are"—the stewardess, reaching her one from a shelf.

Rough and dry the thing was like straw, so she dunked it in the water, then brushed it oozing over an arm. Ah, the warmth, the wet warmth.

She lay back. "Leave me for a little."

"But my queen—"

"Yes, I know. Just for a little. It will be all right, you will see. I'll be ready in time."

The woman went out, sandals slapping.

Then—crystal water blue, shimmering on the ceiling, glancing off the walls.

She ran the sponge along the other arm. Ah, supple and fine; for you, Aigisthos. Then each leg, extending it and working up to the end of the thigh. Slim at the ankle, rounded at the knee; for you too. Then her breasts, soft skin, firm flesh; for you. And finally her middle and the hairy place down there and the little flesh and the other place within. All for you.

Then carefully sliding into the tub even more—to think of it, that yesterday, only yesterday—

.

Dewdrops hanging from every pine needle. The sky is like a morning lake. A shout comes from afar. Then there is a crashing in the brush, and I hear more shouts.

Soon you emerge from among the trees, you with him, the captain, both of you together dragging a huge russet stag with antlers like outspread arms—no, wider.

"Here is dinner!"—the two of you to me, laughing.

I step down to be out of the way and hear—"It's too big"—and "Oof, no, it will just fit, see?"—and "Hah."

Then with a wave the captain drives off, leaving us with linked fingers.

Nearby somewhere sharp-little bells are tingling, and descending we happen upon a limpid stream and an old one there setting out cheese and bread on fig leaves and tempering wine in a gourd shell.

"How goes it, my friend?"

"Well, sir, well," he returns, his voice like a little bird's. Who can they be, he must wonder? Are they Hera and her Zeus? Or perhaps he knows us. "Will you?"—offering us places on his goatskin and to share the meal.

We accept, and oh, the cheese, how smooth it is, and the bread, how coarse; and the wine, it is just right.

He chats with us the while, telling of this year's flock and its fatness and of the shearing to come and of long lost lambs and remarkable dogs that found them.

At length refreshed we rise and thank him.

"And I, you, my lord and lady"—with a little bow.

Again on our way, soon there is a dense wood before us like a pine island. Drowsily we enter it, and in its midst you spread your mantle, and we lie down. Then after a while, we talking and laughing, it becomes very still, as if the birds and other sounding creatures there have all begun to wait for something.

Now your mouth tastes mine and my breasts and there down there, the little flesh, lingering. So that gates, rustic gates, begin to open: one, two, three—a hundred—swinging wide as if in a breeze.

Now my mouth finds yours, and I begin to snuff up your smell—ears, neck, chest—ending with, my mouth aches for it—

Ivory.

And now there is an emptiness in me down there, in there. And I say, "Now. Yes, now." And it quivers in, both of us sighing.

We move slowly at first, then gradually faster and faster, stripping and tossing it all away—

Dead bark from a branchlet when you are a child.

How he will be home soon, my husband. And how if he learns first, he will do everything that he can to bring us grief and bitterness of heart. Yes, he will punish; he may kill.

Until finally all bare and the sweet green within—whip! And the sting and the sting and the sting.

Clasping you to my breast.

Closer.

The hot wetness there within me, yours, mine.

.

But enough. Let there be an end to it, or else I will never get anything done, this bath or anything else.

"Stewardess?" Where is she? The sandals sounded outside the door. So, there. "Come, my back."

The stewardess took up the sponge, and one-two it was done. Then she gave her a hand up and began smoothing the drops from her with a soft cloth.

"What scents are there?"

"Just this, my queen"—bringing down a flask from one of the shelves and showing it.

Rosewater, so be it. And now all dry, she dotted some under her arms, around her breasts, and on the hair, there.

Then the woman helped her back into her robe, and she stepped next door with her. It was a nice room, this one; her husband had had it fitted out for her on the birth of Orestes. Unlike most, it boasted of a window, which made it light and airy. Also you could see the pine forest from it.

And so what shall it be? Or rather what shall I be? For here ranged along the wall on wire and pegs were all of her dress-up clothes: flounced skirts, sheer blouses, and short little jackets. Only I have been wearing a tunic for so long that—"What do you think?"—fingering this-that. But before the woman could open her mouth even—"No. Never mind. I should do this myself."

Well then, what? Obviously the outfit should speak for me, say what I cannot or will not.

To him?

Of course. What?

It needs thinking about. . . .

Hah, there: I'm going to fix you. Try and stop me if you can.

That's not bad. "Bring me some more wine, will you, stewardess." I could do with a little more really.

"Yes, my queen"—going.

Now how or rather with what shall I say it?

Pink is my color. Let that be a beginning. Yes, I shall be a—flower.

All right then, what kind? A rose? A poppy? Something like that?

No, I think not. No, one that never was, I think—or ever shall be, yes. A poisonous one!

Now, the woman having returned with the new goblet, she made her choices, sipping the while: "This"—a skirt, a very full one naturally; "That"—a jacket, really tight-fitting; "This"—an extra-sheer blouse.

Then drawing the filmy thing over her head but keeping the robe wrapped around her hips and her hands and toes buried in the folds—chilly—she sat while the woman worked with brushes, combs, pins, and a ball of black thread to transform the wilderness that was her hair (my man likes it that way) into a row of spitcurls with a diadem along her forehead, a ringlet by each cheek before her ears, and a bun and some braids in the back.

The pine forest, she noted in the meanwhile, was now all

bright green, here and there warm brown earth showing through it. Patience, my man; we will be up there again soon, you will see.

"Do you want to look, my queen?" The woman, with the last piece of thread bitten off, handed her the shining bronze disc.

"Yes." (This, set in an ivory frame with two shapely Heras and a child carved on it, was also a gift from her husband, she recalled, when she had begun to carry Iphigenia.)

She looked. "Nice. Yes. Nice"—that is, from what she could see with it, the rest imagine. The curls and braids, while the standard fashion, fitted in with her notion of the ensemble too, suggesting sprouts and tendrils, especially the latter with their long wispy tapering ends.

Now the woman produced a palette and some little brushes, and she directed her: here black—eyebrows, edge of eyelids, lashes; there white—under brows, the eyes—to make the black stand out; here pink—tender on the cheeks, deeper, almost brownish, on the eyelids, deeper yet, like a raisin, on the lips; and again white—on either side of the nose, around the mouth—to make the pink bloom.

"Well, what do you think?"—with it finished.

The woman considered, tilting her head this-way-that. "It's a little severe, my queen."

"Here, let me see"—taking up the disc. "Suppose that I get dressed"—after examining it. "Then we shall have another look, all right?"

She stood and the woman held the skirt out for her; it was brownish-pink with lighter embroideries, pink too of course, along the flounce edges. Then she put on the jacket, a sort of dusty rose, and slipped into a pair of pale red sandals, the woman stooping to bind them for her.

It needs something more. "Yes, jewelry." But only a little.

The woman brought the box (which matched the disc) and she picked out a strand of gold lilies to go around her neck, a small string for her wrist, and one each, tiny, to dangle from her earlobes.

"What do you think now?"—feeling herself fully dressed and standing back.

"My queen—" The woman gaped. "My queen, it is perfect."

"Yes"—sensing that the jacket was making her back look arched and seeing with eyes down that the tips of her breasts were slightly visible through the blouse and that the skirt, even when she stood very still, seemed to float as if she were being swept along in a breeze, to say nothing of how happily the pale red, brown-pink, almost white pink, and grey-pink blended together. "Yes, I think so too." She took a few tentative steps to see what it was like then. Fine. "So shall we go?"

"Yes, my queen."

But what did we mean by perfect?—as they went out the door, through the corridor, and down, down. Or rather I know what she had in mind, that I looked splendid, maybe even beautiful, but what was in mine? In other words what do I hope to accomplish with it, all this pinkness?

I don't know, or rather I do but cannot quite put it into words.

Did I—do I intend to use it to lure him to be alone with me? Is that it?

It would seem so.

But what about my plan for the beach, the landing?

That was silly, as I see it now. No sooner were I to do it there than his men, all in the heat of the homecoming, would pounce on me, and that would be a sorry end to everything, the two of us lying dead there. Besides, even if I still wanted to, I cannot because I have no knife by me, and there is no time now to find one. No, it is best to do the thing in secrecy. In that way I will have more of a chance of succeeding with it, and then afterward I can tell anyone who wants to know—his men, the captain, the children— exactly what I please, that he became angry with me and tried to harm me in some way . . . something like that.

Let me see, tonight over dinner (chances are there will be a banquet of sorts and I will be required to attend) I will somehow suggest, perhaps even ask him outright, to come and see me later in my chamber, which he will of course, unable to resist flying to such perfection.

Yes, but it must not come to *that*, at least not if I can help it.

And so?

So as soon as he is there, yes, just as he walks through the door, I will—with the knife I will sneak away with me from the table. How is that?

Yes. . . .

Down by the stable she found the captain and the girls— my children—waiting for her, he in the gold chariot, they in another ordinary one. And with the sun yellow-fluttering around, how handsome they seemed, he almost shimmering in his cuirass—though we will both be very hot before the day is out; Elektra in a faun jacket and deep red skirt— curiously like me. Even the little one, her tunic very white, hair—ah, black locks—neatly tied behind.

It is as if we are all about to go on an outing somewhere together.

"Captain"—smiling at him.

"My queen"—with a nod. And he gave the stewardess an approving look.

She turned, smiling still. "Elektra, Chrysothemis."

But neither of them looked her way. Instead Elektra— "Can we go now, captain?"

Ah, my child is impatient, eager to set eyes on her father again; or else—"Elektra?"

The girl still did not pay her any mind, the other one either. And again—"Let us go now, captain, yes?"

So—with a shrug. But then seeing that Elektra had her horse's reins in her hands—no, this is foolish. "Is there no driver for them, captain?"

"I don't want one!"—sharply.

"Elektra!"—this child was unnerving.

"Leave me alone, just leave me alone!"

She let it be—the best thing to do, yes?—and took her place in the chariot, the stewardess, already in, lending her a hand up. "Oh!"—the horse had made a galloping start and she had suddenly fallen backward. Luckily the stewardess caught her, or else everything might have been lost.

"Sorry, my queen"—the captain. Evidently the girl had upset him too.

Now they went more smoothly, and once through the gate and out onto the road she should not have but did turn her head—are they all right, my children?

They were, of course.

Some say that Elektra resembles me, and it may be so, that is, except for her eyes, which are narrower than mine —his, I suppose. But I perceive another there in her face too, someone I know very well but do not quite like. Who is it? My father? Mother? Helen? My brothers? He, he again?

Well, someone . . .

Look! They were entering the town now, and flowers— yellow, light purple, red—seemed to be strung all along the walls there. But it looks as if no one is here—and probably it was so. Yes, they are all gone by now. We will meet some of them on the way. The rest are already there at the beach waiting.

Now they were passing Aigisthos' turn-off. She faced toward where she thought the temple was—I hope you have arrived there without mishap and all is well with you, my man.

Soon, with the last houses behind them, there were people up ahead.

"Make way! Make way!"—the captain.

Instantly, all the way down to its end, it seemed, the road opened—like a flower.

Now they were going by women and children and old ones standing on either side. "Look, look, the queen!"—some, pointing. And once she heard—"Hey, Klytaimnestra, you are beautiful."

You too—she to herself, eyeing their bright happy faces. Still how sad—suspecting (and doubtless it was so) apprehension somewhere deep down in them. For how long would it be before their men, once returned, found out? And how would it happen? Would they hear the tell-tale cry of the infant in its hiding-place? (Fortunately not a problem with me—though she had longed for one, just one, with Aigisthos, especially in the last several years when she had sensed that her time of childbearing was drawing to a close.) Or would someone go and tell them? For almost always there is someone, isn't there? An over-scrupulous neighbor, a witless old one thinking aloud, even a child, unrealizing or resentful.

And here she shouldn't have, surely not again, but did—looked around once more.

They were there, her little ones, only Elektra's eyes still had that hard distant look to them.

Will she ever stop hating us, Aigisthos and me? What have we ever done to her really? Nothing, that is, nothing but good, or at least we tried.

And they had, and how hard they had, both together and singly, and not only to win her friendship but Orestes' as well, for he had followed her in everything.

To think of the times that Aigisthos, on hearing of a foreign ship come in, had gone galloping off to Korinth to look for something nice for her. Once, she recalled, he had brought back (this was long ago) a pretty painted mummy doll with lapis eyes, on another occasion (more recently) a gold seal ring with a fantastic feathery deer carved on it. And then there were those times when he had attempted with promises of high adventure to get the boy to go up to the pine forest with him. But it had all been for naught, and from the very beginning.

Eh, that time, that very first time Elektra had revealed her feelings about them, what a bleak memory.

It had happened several months after his arrival; until then the girl had more or less avoided them, and Orestes had too, of course. Ambling into the courtyard to see the morning, she and Aigisthos had come upon the two of them with one of the boy's playthings, a large bronze bull. Chrysothemis was there also, looking on from the lap of their serving woman.

A few moments before, Elektra (around eleven years old then) had apparently explained how to leap over it, that dark toy, and now Orestes had moved back and was just beginning to run forward.

"No, no, not like that!" Elektra called out.

It was too late. His foot had already tipped it and he was lying on the ground.

At once Aigisthos had gone to him and thrust a hand downward to help him up. "A noble effort, Orestes. You will surely do it the next time."

But Elektra—"My brother does not need your encouragement." Whereupon at a look from her the boy had scrambled up by himself and darted to her side.

Then she, with burning eyes—"We know who you are and want no part of you! You have stolen our father's place. We hate you for it! Would to Hera that he returns soon and finds you!"

Yes, a bleak beginning. Nor did the girl's attitude improve any as time went on. Rather she had grown more bitter yet, her outbursts becoming even more furious, and soon the boy's voice was raised against them as loudly as hers.

One evening some years ago there was a particularly unpleasant scene in the great hall. The two of them had charged in at dinnertime, Elektra screaming at Aigisthos—"You are a usurper and a seducer!"—and Orestes shouting at her, his mother—"And you are a traitress and an adultress!" There was nothing for it but to separate the two of them. So the next day, acting on a suggestion of the captain's, she had packed the boy off to Phokis and its king, one Strophios, a special friend of Agamemnon's.

But such a step appeared to have no effect on Elektra. Or rather it did, but not in the way intended. The scenes in the great hall had continued, and soon with Orestes not around she had turned her attention to little Chrysothemis, no longer a baby.

Sometime last spring (that is, before news of the victory had reached them) Aigisthos had come up with an idea about Elektra's fury—that it really had little if anything to do with resentment. But so curious had been his notion of what the real trouble was, that she had found it hard to accept—still did.

One night the girl had tried something incredibly foolish, rushing away after denouncing them in the great hall to the rampart in the courtyard to fling herself into the ravine below. Luckily Aigisthos and the captain, who happened to be present then, had sensed something—I did not—and chased after her and caught hold of her just in time. Then, very concerned, Aigisthos had carried her crying, a child, up to her chamber himself. And it was then, on his return from there, that he mentioned it, though probably it had been on his mind for some time already.

"But I don't understand"—had been her response. "Elektra is so harsh to you all the time. How can she be that way and also as you say?" Had the girl done something to indicate it?

No, not really, he admitted. It was just a feeling that he had.

Still, supposing that it was so, what could they have done about it, found someone and married her off to him? No, I could not do that to her regardless of how she might feel toward me; no, not to a child of mine—never. And I made that very clear to Aigisthos.

So there the matter had rested, the two of them hoping against hope that if that really were the trouble, Elektra would somehow or other resolve it or at least not try anything harmful against herself again. . . .

And now? Now it looks as if the girl is ready to let her father know everything and at the first opportunity, which might very well happen down there on the beach.

Can I do anything about it?

I wish I knew. Ah, maybe the captain has an idea. "My daughter is a little out of sorts today, wouldn't you say, captain?"

He seemed absorbed in managing the reins.

"Will she be all right, do you think?"

"We shall see, my queen."

I don't understand. Doesn't the man realize the danger? And not only to me but to himself and her too, his stewardess. What have you been doing all these years, my husband is bound to demand. Do you mean to tell me that in all that time you did not have a single chance to try anything? Oh surely he must see that. Or if he has not yet—but maybe he has—he will soon, I know it. He is no fool.

And when he does, hopefully before very long, if I cannot prevent the girl from telling just then, maybe he or even his woman will be able to.

Now with a breeze, the faintest sea breeze, in her nostrils, she recalled how once on a very hot day long ago, just after her return from Aulis, he and the stewardess had put her in a cart and driven to the shore with her. Then how on reaching there, he had helped her down and set her on a pallet and the stewardess had spread a cool wet cloth on her forehead.

Conscious of riding along with them on either side of her again and indeed to the very same place, she felt somehow refreshed and stood straight with this new strength.

·

What? Looking back at us? How dare she?—Elektra, in her chariot.

You wait till my father comes; he'll show you! Doing it over and over again with that Aigisthos. Why even this morning probably, yes, even then she was at it. His juices are probably still dribbling there down the inside of her thighs. Unless in the bath— Never mind. You just wait! And—"*Whack!*"—she went with the whip. The horse gave a skip, hurting.

"Please, sister, have patience"—the little one, her voice a sad bell.

Patience? She wants me to have patience? No! No! No! No! That woman who calls herself our mother must be punished right away, as soon as my father gets off the ship. She is dirt; yes, that is just what she is, dirt.

But my sister is right; I shouldn't get so upset. I feel light in the head now. And there, down there, mine, it is beginning to— Yes, again; for she had done it that morning too. Six times. I thought my arm would fall off. Only still not enough. Never was, never seemed to be.

And quickly her hand shot down and grabbed it there and gave it, ah, a good squeeze, then jumped away again before little prying eyes could see.

Where can I go?—peering round. There seemed to be people everywhere.

I know; I will drive off the road and in among the trees until I'm out of sight.

I wonder if I can do it by rubbing it up against one of them, its bark. How nice if I were able to sharpen it and make it pointy at the same time. Then maybe I could stick this baby with it. I'd like that—in even just a little.

What would she do? Whine, I suppose; that's how she usually acts when I do something to her. Stop it, Elektra, you're hurting me! Hur—ting me! Her mouth always smells so of milk.

But what am I about? There is no time for that right now. I have to be there when my father gets in. Yes, that first. "So on!"—making the horse skip again.

"Please, sister!"

Eh, the milk. Nevertheless, she reined the beast in some.

Yes, my father will take care of you, I promise you—her gaze firmly fixed once more ahead on her mother. Aigisthos too, when he gets hold of him, which he will.

And before that he will torture you, both of you. I don't know how, but he will. He'll think of something. And when he does— Oh I can't wait to see the pain in your eyes and hear you scream. Yes, you even more than he, your dribbler.

Obviously you expect it too and are terrified, going to meet him all fancied-up like that. He also, running away to hide among a bunch of women.

I always suspected that there was something cowardly about him, yes, even in spite of how sure of himself he always is.

That night, for instance, when he carried me to my chamber. "I'm sorry," he said, and how he shook. I could feel it through his hand when it touched my arm then.

Well, now it is confirmed, his fearfulness; yes, from now on he is nothing but a boy in my eyes.

Like the one he sent me the next day. Yes, that is what he did. The following morning there was this fellow from the garrison at my door telling me that the prince had sent him to ask how I fared. Can you imagine it?

And he was a boy, big as he was (which he was too, almost as lumpy as the captain), and I sensed it at once. Then when I motioned for him to come closer and pulled up his tunic, I knew it for certain. What did he have there in the middle of the hairs (and there weren't many of them either) but a—well, it was like a little thumb.

Still I showed that Aigisthos. I told his boy, in fact commanded it as his princess, that he should get it ready, what was there, with his hand. And when he did (it was still not much, like a small arrow), I told him to keep on doing it until its juices came out, which I must say was rather silly, the way it shot up from the hole there on the tip and arched around like a fountain. After this I made him get on the bed with me and used his hand to rub it up, mine, until—

Ice-streaks! It was the best! The best ever! I swear it!

Then I gave him a push, a good hard one, so he fell on the floor. And dragging him up by the hair, I told him not to breathe a word of what he had done to anyone or I would go down there to the garrison house and before everyone, all his friends, chop it off for him, that stupid thing of his.

He went away with tears in his eyes. "Har! Har!" . . .

What again? Is Her Foulness looking here again? Why— And for a moment it was as if her father were already there.

If only I had something by me now, even an old broken knife, I would do it myself and save him the trouble. I would.

How many times lying in her chamber at night alone, almost suffocating there, so close was it, had she longed to do just that, especially when her mother and Aigisthos were together, and he was dribbling it.

And once long ago she nearly had, though it was not to be quite like that. Aigisthos had disappeared somewhere with the captain that day. Orestes (they had made it up) was to go and find her, the dirty woman. Then while he distracted her with his childish chatter, his big sister would creep up on her from behind with the little sword. Only when the time came, he had begun to boo-hoo, the baby. So she had been obliged to give his toy back to him.

But he would not behave like that today, I expect. Oh no, not now—now that he is a man. . . .

After my father has taken care of the two of them, he will do by me as he should, find someone suitable for me to marry, the son of a high-king with a good citadel and a fine palace, yes, the same as he would have for Iphigenia.

Now there was something. Can you imagine the tainted one being upset over that? Why it was a pure and holy act, what my father did. It will never be forgotten. All of Greece will honor it forever and ever. We others, I and Orestes and even the milk here, would have jumped at the chance, as I am sure she herself did, gentle Iphigenia, had he chosen one of us instead! . . .

What was I thinking?

Oh yes, my marriage.

But before that, before my father attends to that, he should bring my brother back. Yes, yes, Orestes comes first.

And that! Imagine sending him, still a little boy really, so far away from home. Cruel it was.

Unnatural!

After Orestes' return, sooner or later my father will grow weary and, wanting only to roam the pine forest, give over the rule to him. Then one day I, his older married sister, will come visiting him here. And oh, the joy when I leap

from my chariot into his arms and we go running off together to one of those rooms where we used to play and
talk them all over, the old times.

Later, before the end of our stay, my husband and I will
propose giving Orestes a little help. For he cannot go on
like that, a grown man, we will feel; he absolutely must
marry. Who knows, it may turn out that my husband has a
younger sister, if not, then a cousin, no matter really—

But now there was something on the road ahead, as the
captain was slowing down, and she had to too.

What is it? What can it be?

Then she heard—

Aie, Aie, Aie
Aie, Aie, Aie

Eh, yellow fluff, his women, the fugitive-seducer's.

Captain, do something, will you. For I must see my father when he arrives. Everything depends on it.

"Hurry"—under her breath. "Get them off the road."

Do it, or I'll grab something, a sword or something, and
kill everyone!

.

"They will not yield the way, my queen"—the captain.

"Go around them then."

Not having laid eyes on the like since the men all went
off to the war, Klytaimnestra, supported by the stewardess,
looked the party over curiously as her chariot rocked by it
on the road's shoulder. A pretty creature, the heifer, what
with its shining dark eyes and pinkish nose. And how well-
matched they are, the yellow-swaying girls; all of the same
height, it would seem. As for the three in the cart, truly
with their pure fair skin and black black eyes and hair, to
say nothing of their utterly even features, they appeared to
be of one flesh.

The elder, the perfect mother or rather grandmother, gave her a smile as if to say—yes, he is with us, your man, and yes, we shall keep him for a time.

She smiled back—I'm glad, but it won't be for long, I assure you. In a while, a little while, I will have him once more, you will see.

Now they were on the road again and ahead of the holy group. Better. It makes one feel uneasy being around them for long. They are almost too fine.

Soon there was more of a breeze, and they began passing loinclothed youths lolling under trees with wineskins. She heard their still new deep voices—how easily they laugh.

A little further on there were boys; they seemed to be everywhere, kicking up dust, hollering from branches. And then around the next bend there it was, water, and hugging every shady nook by it were stark reds and yellows and blues and greens and oranges.

Why it is a garden—of women!

She allowed the captain to help her down and get her settled, a few of his men having preceded them in carts with stools and things.

And the girls? She turned around. So. He was seating them right behind her. Elektra? Her eyes seemed as before —no, not quite: there was a trace of satisfaction in them now.

She looked away toward the bay. No sign of anything there yet, still too early.

But how disappointing it is, the water. It seems tepid, stale somehow. And the sky, she noted, was now all hot white, the sun, directly overhead, a glaring white ball.

"My queen?"—the stewardess, with a cup.

"Water? All right"—accepting it. She took a swallow and held the cup poised for another.

If she tries to tell him here and one of us manages to prevent it (which may not be as difficult as it might seem;

after all doesn't he have more important things to do than stand around prating with a child and a female one at that), she must not get another chance. That means the thing must be done tonight without fail.

In which case I must make absolutely certain that he comes to me in my chamber later.

Suppose I tell him while we're dining that I have something to say for his ears alone about Orestes, whom he will have missed here and about whom the captain will have furnished only a cursory explanation. That should certainly bring him—that is, if my charms fail to.

But I must not forget to take a knife along with me as I get up to go. . . .

And I will have to hold it in such a way that it cannot be seen. . . .

There is still another problem. How do I know that quick as I will be to wield it, he, a man, a soldier, will not be quicker.

It might come to *that* then.

No.

Yes. I could be there in bed with the knife by me, hidden of course, and then when he—

No, I couldn't.

Not even for Aigisthos, so that we can spend the rest of our life together?

I don't think so.

It may be the only sure way of getting it done.

In that case— But what about Orestes and the information?

Later, it can wait until later, I will tell him when he appears. Right now, not having seen him in so long (and I will hold a hand out to him so, lying there), I want to—

But won't this eagerness of mine seem strange after everything that has passed between us?

Not at all. On the contrary.

Even so he may not want to or be able to. Maybe he will be too tired from her, his captive.

I doubt it. They have been on the sea for some time, and one does not do it there, I think; there is no privacy. No, he will be fresh in that respect, I am almost sure.

Well, if that really is the only way. But how shall I—

Aha. First I will let him do it. Then, when he has (which will not take very long, yes?), just at the moment when his head is low, by my neck, I will grasp it, the knife—and strike as hard as I can!

Stick it into him—in the back there!

At Sea

———

— *IV* —

"It is not much further"—Agamemnon, in the prow, re-calling a certain inlet and promontory that they were leaving behind.

No one seemed to care. His men just sat as they had all morning, by their oarlocks with their heads down. And in the other ships, he noted, looking here and there, it was more or less the same.

It will be different later, when we are in the bay, I think. And with his feet planted firmly on the planks, he let himself rock along some more, relishing it but not the sun, which was burning hot, especially on the back of the neck during the wind lulls.

After a time he could not help it—"Almost!" He had recognized a family of jutting rocks and another promontory.

Then soon it happened. The breeze that had been nudging them suddenly quickened, giving them a strong push, and, lo, there was Nauplion, sheer citadel, looming on their right and ahead in the distance like the twin pillars of a giant gate those of Argos and Tiryns, and far below them just barely visible—though there!—the landing-place. "Look!"—with a sweep of his arm. "Look, home!"

The men, most of them, raised their heads and seeing that it was really so, began talking among themselves. Now if only I can get them to take up the oars.

But that was not to be. Almost at once their shoulders dropped down and they lapsed into silence once more. Well, that is all right too; I will try them again later. The wind can do the work for the present—it was still blowing nicely. Yes, let them go on resting now, my poor men.

For it had been a long voyage and hard too. In fact so trying had they found it that now on thinking it over (there was time to now), he wondered if it had not all been the work of some spirit. Not you of course, Hera. But maybe it was one of those Trojan goddesses or gods bent on revenge or just plain mischief.

Still, Hera, what were you doing while we were catching it out there? Were you napping or something? Surely you could not have observed us suffering so without providing a little relief.

Yes, it was very pleasant at first. Were you looking on then? You were? Well, so was that same spirit, I suspect, and smilingly to disarm us of our fears. For now on my recollecting, once we left the dead walls of Troy behind and sailed past Tenedos, mute island, it was almost too much so.

Ah, the coast of Mysia, the shore of Lesbos. Every morning we would run to the ships, hoist the sails, and a good stern-wind always with us, ride along until it suited us to do so no more. Then we made for shore and bagged something for our dinner (usually without any great ado, game was plentiful on either hand), and then while the men took their slaves behind the hulls, I would draw her off, my captive, deep into the woods where we could not be seen and spread my mantle for us.

Nor was this the end of our cheery time. Later on, gathered round the campfires, we would fill our bellies up good and then settle back and listen, nodding, as the harpers sang of what already seemed like long ago and far away— how after many a year of hard battle Achilleus, our best, bettered theirs, Hektor; then how the city still resisting, Odysseus, crafty in mind and body, came up with the trick of the horse statue for gaining access; and with this done how I, Agamemnon, shepherd of shepherds, led everyone to victory. Afterward, fondly musing on our fine treasures —mine, theirs—we would fall off into a deep and lasting sleep.

Then in no time at all, it seemed, came the day for the wide crossing. And that Trojan deity, she or he, must still have been grinning, for we accomplished this without mishap and easily. Nor did we at first meet with any difficulty when beginning to run down our own coast. But then, no sooner did Sounion dip below the horizon and the long arm of Argolis—home—sweep into view, than, oh Hera, the sky grew black and the sea swelled so, it looked as if it were going to gobble everything up, and such a wind arose that in a moment almost every mast had snapped and ships were foundering everywhere. Truly, with my own spinning round and round, punched furiously on every side, or else shooting uncontrollably forward I thought that our end had come.

But what do you think, Hera? All at once the wind abated, indeed as suddenly as it had come up, and the sky grew clear, the sea fell, and relieved, we pointed what ships of ours remained homeward again.

As it was to turn out, this storm was only our first trial. And the next, when it came soon after, seemed even more severe. We were aware of what was about to happen but could do nothing whatsoever about it.

It was my captive (leaving her place in the stern to do so) who first called our attention to it, though of course we had been hearing it too for some time without realizing it.

Then a large wave came and lifted us up and we saw—Maleia!—we were all heading straight for the giant rock-tooth.

Instantly everyone jumped to do something. Some began rowing, many of them so hard that the oars broke or slipped from their hands. Others went and flung everything their eyes discovered overboard—war gear, the hard-won treasures, even slaves—so that in moments the water around us was teeming with heads and things, and women were moaning there and children screaming, ah.

In spite of all these efforts we were no further away from the ship-smasher. In fact, with the current pushing us in that direction and the confusion everywhere, some may even have gotten closer to it, so that once more, Hera, I thought that it was all over for us.

But just at the last moment, it seemed, yes, just as with the storm, the current stopped; and then almost at once it moved again, but the other way, so that we were sent back whence we had come. And on the current went like that for what remained of that day and well into the night.

This should have been the end of our troubles, for we had suffered enough, don't you agree? But that Trojan had yet one more trial in store for us, and this one, Hera, oh, my insides begin to churn at the thought of it.

The next morning we found ourselves on a still sea with no land in sight and no provisions to speak of.

I immediately had what little there was portioned out and, ordering the other ships to do the same (there were now some sixty out of the original hundred), set them all to rowing in what I judged to be the right direction. But soon, in the next day or so, everything—all the barley and water and wine too—was consumed, and on the following days the pouches and skins, and after that our sandals, sword-straps, and whatever. It was a wonder that we did not then fall on the slaves that were still with us. We were too weak by that time, I suppose. And needless to say, what with the sun forever beating on everyone's head, gradually the rowing slowed and then ceased altogether.

Finally there came what seemed like our last moments. The sky, I recall, was unusually pale that afternoon and all around us sharks were waiting, chasing the while after our dirt, the little of it that still issued from our bodies.

Realizing that we were all about to die there then, I became very sad, regretting that I would never see my son again and have a chance to launch him in the world, and that the men—my brave men—after so many years on the battlefield were going to perish in this way, so stupidly and on the voyage home.

And it was then, Hera, that you must have opened your eyes and learned and taken pity on us (at least that is what I like to believe happened). Maybe you even told the other, that Trojan, a thing or two—she had tortured your son enough, let him be. For a little later on that day a breeze arose, bringing with it some clouds and a light rain. Then no sooner had we moistened our mouths with it than we seemed to be surrounded by hundreds and hundreds of fish, these small and tame enough for us to grab hold of with our bare hands. And finally, the breeze freshening somewhat as the light faded—this will bring us in, I told myself.

And so it happened. Early this morning, lo, there was land again lying dark-bluish on both sides of us, that is, until the signal fires—fine golden beads—began to stretch along it. Then the sun, a precious golden eye, came up—

Some of the men had begun to stir again. "Look! Look!" —they were pointing ahead.

He did and saw. With their further progress the landing place was clearly visible now, and he could make out specks there. No mistaking it, people were waiting.

She is among them, of course, still angry with me probably, and one cannot blame her. Still she is my wife, she will be there.

The children too, I'm sure; she has seen to that. Orestes— Eh, he must be grown up by now.

Will he take part in the games, I wonder?

Yes? What will he do—run, jump, throw the stone, or what?

All of them? Good.

For there would be games of course. After all what is a homecoming, no matter how sluggish one feels (though I don't, I think), without a little friendly sport? And a feast afterward for my leaders. Anyway that is how Atreus used to have it when he came home, as I recall—first games, then a banquet—so that is how it will be with me, his son.

Except I have forgotten about the thanksgiving. Yes, that comes first, before these. Forgive me, Hera.

What—what should I say then?

And he would have tried to think up something. But just then there was a presence by him. That is my captive I suspect. He gave a sideways glance—so it is. All morning long she had lain in her place back there showing as little interest in everything as the men. But now having heard their outcry, she had become curious apparently.

"Are we there?"

"Yes"—he, with his eyes back on the land, though there was nothing further to see yet as the specks were only slightly larger.

She stood and gazed with him for a while. Then—"What will become of me after?"

A good question. What should I do with her now that we are safe and almost there? Obviously something, but I don't know what yet. "We shall see."

"But—"

"Soon, we shall see soon."

And they would. He would think of something; it would come to him in a little. . . .

Eh, the girls, they were the best part of the war. And remembering, he could not help making a big grin.

There had been two others before this one: Chryseis and Briseis. It sounded as if they were twins or sisters, but they were not, no, not in any respect.

Chryseis. Now there was a girl who was so slippery-wet inside that when you put your phallus in, you had to hold it there like a stick in water, or—heh-heh—it would jump right out again. Achilleus had captured her in a raid on Chryse, where her father was the high priest of Apollo she had boasted. But so full of fun did she turn out to be in addition to everything else that everyone including himself had not taken this claim very seriously, at least at first.

Ah Chryseis, always singing and dancing and banging on her cauldrons with her ladles and spoons while she cooked. And the things she used to say sometimes. Why once—har! —pausing in the middle of one of her performances, she had pointed those great milky breasts of hers at him and— "Hey, high-leader, the Trojans are coming." Then there was the time when he was about to ride off in his war gear with his men—"Take care that the Trojans do not make it shorter, my dear. I shall miss it sore—ly." And once when she had gone too far and waked the whole camp screaming that the Trojans were there and killing her and he had given her a good whiplash for it, what did she do—har!— but stick her bottom out again and—"Oh, that felt good. Do it some more please."

One day an old one in a robe full of orange and pink suns had showed up and claiming to be her father offered something (though not much) in ransom for her. But he, the high-leader, had sneered at him and sent him packing, and what a mistake that had turned out to be.

The next morning the whole camp, including the horses

and dogs, was green and vomiting, and by evening there had even been a number of deaths. So I had to send the frisky girl after her old one, with presents no less, the other leaders—Nestor, Idomeneus, the two Aiases, and the rest—insisting on it to the point of giving everything up and going home.

And who had instigated it all? Who had caused them to become so fearful-cautious all of a sudden? Who else but that troublemaker Achilleus. The plague was Apollo's doing, he had told them, and unless the holy man got his girl back and was placated in some other ways the god would not stop until he had destroyed them all.

A lot he knew!

But I showed him, the upstart, didn't I, Hera? For it was not right that the high-leader should be the only one without a woman—so I let them all know, Achilleus included. And since the young man had been so willing to part with what did not belong to him, it was only right that the replacement should come from him and his.

And that was how he had acquired Briseis, another of Achilleus' captives, this one from Lyrnessos where her father truly was a high priest (of Dionysos). The most interesting thing about it was that possessing another (would you believe it, an older one, like a mother) Achilleus had not gotten around to doing it to this one yet.

But this venture had a slight setback, huh, Hera? For when my men went to get her from Achilleus he let them have her all right, but then he sat down in front of his hut and refused to go out and fight anymore. And soon missing him in the field, the others made me give Briseis back to him, to say nothing of all manner of gifts and promises of more with the victory. To make matters worse I also had to swear before them all that I had never touched her in that way.

Even so it did not turn out badly in the end, did it?

Suspecting that something of the kind might happen (did you perhaps warn me in a dream, Hera?) and that he might even turn her upside down (which he did) to see if what I had sworn was so, I never did do it to her either. Instead—

Ah, she had the nicest thickest lips, that Briseis. And how her eyes bulged out (stupid blue they were) when I made her swallow it.

Yes, I got the best of him after all, that Achilleus! . . .

This one here, while a captive too, was different from the others, not only because of her lineage (she was Priam's child by his wife, Hekabe) but also how she came to him (by lot in the general sharing-out on the morning after the city fell—therefore through you, Hera). There was something else that was distinctive about her, though exactly what, it was hard to say.

Perhaps it has to do with the fact that she is very small—nose, mouth, all over—indeed like a child.

Possible, but I'm not sure.

Well, then?

I don't know; does it matter?

Still he could not let it be.

They had brought her to his hut that morning, as it happened in rather sad condition. It seems that during the excitement of the previous night, what with Odysseus and those with him quitting the horse and the rest of them piling into the city from without, someone had come upon her in the Athena temple and either because he did not know or care the inevitable had occurred. And so it had been useless to go to her that day, for she lay, so his steward reported, like one dead.

But the next day was another matter. The city and the palace were pretty well gutted (even the smoke had more or less cleared away by then) and the other leaders, who had done it to their prizes at least once, talked of making for home now, but he had wanted his turn. So that afternoon he had stopped by to see for himself what was what with her.

There was some kind of ruckus going on in the next hut at the time, he recalled. Someone, a female voice, was imploring; others, men, laughing. And on his captive's request (it had annoyed him a little too) he had gone over to make them quiet down.

A young girl was there, not more than ten years old he guessed. Two of his men had her cowering in a corner and were reeling toward it. And seeing that one or both of them had already done it to her (she was bleeding) and that in all likelihood it was over for her, a child, in her head anyway, he had taken his sword and put an end to their cruel fun.

Then, with it hushed, he had returned to his own hut and her. But now there was something else the matter, or rather it was the same thing. For on his standing there and looking down at her, try as he might, he could not get the other one, her bleeding and his men closing in on her, out of his head. And then noticing her smallness (perhaps she was afraid too, so quietly had she lain there) and recalling that not long ago someone had done it to her in that way too, all at once he had begun to shake.

He had experienced such spells before of course, though normally they were much worse, with sweating everywhere, especially the head and hands, a haziness about the eyes, and a sinking feeling inside. They usually came on after some particularly bad turn of events in the field, as, for instance, that time when because of Achilleus' sulk, Hektor and his men were about to break through their defenses and get at the camp and the ships. So he had known enough from those other times to take a little walk for himself, this being the only sure way to make it pass. Then deciding during the course of it to let it be for a while (perhaps he would try it later that day or the next one, before they sailed, or even afterward along the way, when they stopped off, there was no hurry really), he had gone back to—to— for some reason he could not recall.

They had spoken for a few moments, she asking after the fate of her family and he answering as best he could. Then with nothing further to say, he had noticed that she was now looking at him differently, as if she—he didn't know. Except that of a sudden his phallus had given a jump, and the next moment he was on top of her and her legs had opened of their own and they had both then together sought the place to put it.

Sought and found, no more. His juices had left him almost at once. Yes, it was all gone in her, poured there in an instant.

Whereupon he had wanted to get up and go away again. Only—what was this?—she would not let him, no, had kept him there, pressing him with her hands from behind. Nor could he break her hold. For when he had tried— what did she want? What was she after?—what had she done but dug her nails into the skin.

Finally, though, she had given a groan. And when she did, it had gripped him and so hard that he—yes, again.

Only it was like bleeding then. Yes, yes, that time he had bled-bled-bled it all—imagine it, there was more—into her! . . .

Now sensing her presence anew—so it is in that respect that she differs from those others. Yes, that is it. And so once again what should I do with her?

I could put her in the servant's quarters, I suppose. That is what one usually does with captives. Then one can go and visit them whenever one cares to. Atreus must have had an arrangement like that, maybe more than one, though I can't remember them.

But what would my wife think of it? She is angry with me as it is. Won't it make matters worse with her?

Eh, who cares!

I must not say that; it is not right. She is the mother of my son.

I guess the best thing to do then is to give her to one of my farmers or shepherds. Of course I can still get to see her now and again if I have a mind to; all one has to do is send the husband away on an errand somewhere. . . .

Well, let it go for now; can't think about it anymore. Later. Yes, I'll do it later, once we are there or maybe even after that—there is no rush—tomorrow. She can stay here in the ship tonight. I'll decide tomorrow.

For if it had been a bad voyage, it was a worse war. Do you remember, Hera? It was, wasn't it, worse, the war? . . .

The saddest thing about it was that it had all seemed so simple talking it over with Odysseus there in Tyndareos' woods. All he, the new high-king of Mykenai, had to do was get the father to agree to the matches, which was easy enough (it would be either as I wanted it or not at all), and then once the old fool was out of the way and the young ones had taken his place, sit back and with a little care at the right time, seeing to it that Menelaos was drawn off to Pylos before Paris turned up and so on, the rest would follow as eventually a bright day a gloomy one.

Indeed at first everything had gone well, he and Odysseus having judged correctly about how much Paris wanted to do it to her, Helen, and that given the chance he would stop at nothing for it, even violate the rules of guest-friendship. Nor had they been far from the mark regarding Paris' elder brother Hektor, who thought himself a regular Zeus with a spear and seemed always on the lookout for chances to prove it, and old Priam, who, doting on them both, was usually eager to go along with their enterprises even when not altogether sanguine about their wisdom. True, there were problems, as when Palamedes so ingratiated himself with Priam on "poor Menelaos' behalf" during the first embassy as to threaten to ruin everything on the next one. But these were usually handled with ease. In the case of Palamedes, for instance, since he would not hear of being left out of the negotiations, they had no choice (regrettably because of the long-standing connection between the two families) but to get rid of him. And he, the high-leader, had made the accusation before the others, using the forged letters from Priam and Trojan gold that Odysseus had hidden in the man's hut.

But then, Hera, came that business with my daughter, and I still do not understand why it was necessary. You did not want her blood; I know it. Nor did any of your fellow gods. No, it was the other leaders, only they did.

And the reason? I don't know. It sounded so odd. They told me that they felt I ought to do it as a gesture to show that I had their interests at heart as well as my own, meaning Menelaos', I suppose.

But how could they have thought otherwise? Didn't they realize that I needed them, that the success of the whole venture regardless of how one looked at it depended on them?

I wonder now. Is it possible that someone was going around behind my back planting false suspicions in their minds? Someone like that Achilleus, for instance, yes, even then scheming how to make me uncomfortable?

But what difference now? No, it doesn't matter anymore. It was a bad business regardless of who was really responsible. And as you may recall, Hera—oh, how could one forget!—after that nothing seemed to go right.

How many times on our first arriving before Troy did we fight them fiercely on the plain for a few days and then, our scouts the next morning reporting no activity within, go racing up to the walls only to be greeted by their bowmen rising from the silence. And how many times if we remained there long enough, which we often had no choice about, so thick and fast was the rain of arrows, did their spearmen and chariots come bursting on us as suddenly from the gates. After a while it seemed as if it would go on forever, our being tricked in that way and then, when we found their forces again waiting for us out on the plain, having to start all over with a new battle.

Even in the end, after Hektor and most of their best men were gone and their allies could not or would not help anymore and the last of the adventure seekers, Penthesilea of Pontus and her troop of women, Memnon of Aithiopia and his black men—the one charging us on horseback with swinging axes and shrilling all the time, the other with painted faces and in leopard pelts loping after our chariots with spears and arrows flying—even after they had come and tried and failed, the city would not give in; its bowmen led by Paris still kept us at a respectful distance from the walls.

Nor was this unyielding of the Trojans all that we had to contend with, Hera. There was also (even now I begin to shiver remembering it) day after day of greyness and gloom throughout the year, with more often than not a fierce downpour or in winter icy sleet and grisly snow. Why even our contingents from the north had never experienced anything like it.

This created muck everywhere and all the time, and everything—horses, chariots, mules, carts, even men (I can still hear them cursing)—was forever getting stuck in it. It was a wonder that we ever reached the city at all, came back too.

Also once something got wet, we soon learned, it never seemed to dry out again. When you got up in the morning, even after a fire had been going all night, you were chilled through and through, and each breath that you took was like a gulp. Sometimes the first few seemed like your last.

Worst of all of course was what happened to a wound,

even a minor one, because of the clamminess. Almost overnight a gashed limb would turn all grey and numb and the man to whom it belonged would be horribly dead in a day or so. Several mornings after every engagement there were corpses, blackish and bloated, all over the camp, and as the day wore on their number grew, until it was impossible to build pyres fast enough. And, oh, the smell everywhere then. You would not believe it unless you had been there.

Still, trying as these were, our stubborn opponent and his weather, they were nothing compared to what I—I alone—had to endure besides. Wouldn't you say, Hera?

That Achilleus, for instance, what a nuisance he was to begin with; I knew it as soon as I laid eyes on him at Aulis. But later on, especially after I gave him his Briseis back and he got all those gifts and promises out of me, he became almost impossible, either flying into a flutter or else wailing and whining about something or other, and this nine-times-out-of-ten turned out to be a trifle.

Like that time when they brought his special friend's Hektor-ridden body back—what was his name? Ah, Patroklos. Why I've never heard of a grown man carrying on, hugging and kissing one like that.

Then there was the way he treated Hektor when he caught up with him (I could almost say, poor Hektor), making him kneel and beg for his life, then running him through and hitching the corpse to his chariot and dragging it round the city all the way to the camp and Patroklos' pyre (so he could have a look too, I suppose, wherever he thought his spirit might be).

And how he howled when his turn came, Achilleus. Why I wouldn't be surprised if our enemy heard him in the innermost recesses of the palace. Imagine it, all because of a little arrow in the foot (though of course we had no way of knowing at the time that the thing was poisoned).

Even when dead Achilleus did not cease to be a bother. Now that was bad. While bearing his body back to the camp, Odysseus and big Aias of Telamon had a falling out over who got the armor, and when they brought the matter before the others Odysseus was given the vote. Aias went away upset and the next day we were making a pyre for him, our other mainstay. After the hearing he had returned to his hut and taken his sword and fallen on it.

But the worst thing that Achilleus did, far worse than all of these put together, was to turn the others against me. This he did not only by challenging my authority in their presence as in the case of Chryseis but also by whispering things about me to them behind my back, which he must have been doing all along. For though a little cool to me toward the end there at Aulis, everyone was much more so once we landed at Troy and the fighting started, to the point where they all began interfering with me and what was supposed to be my business. And to the best of my knowledge I never gave them cause for this loss of confidence in me.

Unfortunately, my sensing it when I did had a bad effect on me. I don't know why, but I couldn't seem to help myself and actually began showing poor judgment on occasion, yes, as if to confirm those worst feelings of theirs. And now and again, I confess it, the result was a serious blunder on my part.

Like that time Hektor was about to get at us behind our wall and Achilleus started packing up his gear. I told them all in the council house that sooner than give in to Achilleus and his moodiness we ought to go home too. How they looked at me then, Hera. Even Odysseus, the very best of special friends, was furious with me and he shouted it out in front of all of them.

I was sorry. . . .

After that, during the last year or so, they all took to
ignoring me more or less completely and relying on Odysseus for the conduct of the war. But, as I saw it, only when
it suited them. For instance, after Achilleus and Aias were
gone, they came up with the idea of trying to reduce the
number of Trojans on the walls at long distance but did not
have an accurate enough marksman for the job. So they
sent Odysseus to find one, which he did (on Lemnos, I
believe). Then when this succeeded somewhat, the archer
managing to pick off a few of them up there including
Paris, and still the enemy hung on (now with another
brother, Deiphobos, giving the orders), they charged Odysseus to go over to Thessaly and bring back Achilleus' son,
Neoptolemos (who was little more than a boy but reputedly
almost as big and strong as his father had been), and go
ahead with the building of the horse statue. For lack of a
better scheme they would give it a try.

Except that on adopting it they had the notion—can you
imagine it—that I would stay in the thing with Neoptolemos while they together with Odysseus hid at Tenedos until
we got out of it and opened the city gates for them. But no,
I told them, when they summoned me to inform me of this,
I would have none of it. Odysseus dreamt the horse up, so
let him go and sit in it. And what could they do; I meant
what I said.

That was a blunder too, I suppose. But since they were
already good and fed up with me by that time, it couldn't
have made any difference, could it, Hera?

After it was all over, on the second day after the sharing-
out, I woke to find the beach empty, that is, except for my
ships (and Odysseus' too). Apparently all of them had
risen and sailed off very early, for the sun had just come up.
They had not even waited to say goodbye—Nestor, who in

the beginning had been almost like a father to me, Idomeneus and the other Aias, brothers, Diomedes too, whose high-king I was, and even my own Menelaos, who had always listened to me in everything.

As for Odysseus, he had not finished loading his stuff yet. Besides, he was not going home, at least not just then, he told me when I sought him out. There would still be room left in his ships he had calculated, so he had decided to do a little raiding up in Thrace first.

He even asked me if I would care to go along with him. But when I saw that his eyes were avoiding mine I suspected that he didn't mean it. Oh well, I didn't want to anyway. . . .

And now? Now I don't need them anymore, any of them. No, not even Odysseus. For now (his eyes actively scanned the shore again and made out that those there were all waving) I am home, and whom do they greet in this way but me, their high-king.

A little group with a reddish blur in its midst stood by itself on the left side. Is that she perhaps? Then one of the others must be Orestes.

If only Atreus could be there too—he pictured his dark grey eyes and lean muscularity. But no, he is not. He is gone for good and I must not fall to wishing for what cannot be.

Ah, he was a fine man. They say that he killed my mother, but I can scarcely believe that. No, Thyestes did it out of spite or something, I am almost sure of it. I owe all that I know to him, to Atreus, yes—the sword, the bow, the light spear, the heavy—everything. And he had sound advice to offer to a young man. Try it out with an older woman first, he had suggested. Yes, no question about it, my father gave me a good start in this world.

And soon, once we are there and everything has settled

down, I will begin passing on what he taught me to my son; that is, if it is not too late, which I trust that it will not be....

He could almost see them plainly now, those people on the land. So it is time, I think. I will give the signal and hopefully my men will see it and go to work with the oars—of course they will—and we will make a nice show.

But now just as he was about to raise his arm it was stayed by the hand of his captive. "Something is wrong!"

What? He looked down at her. "Where?"

"There"—her eyes ahead on the shoreline.

He followed but found nothing, nothing, that is, that he had not already noted: the eager crowd, the reddish blur. "What is it?"

"I don't know, something."

"Something?" But what? His eyes returned there, going over everything again, this time very slowly, only with the same result—nothing.

"Yes"—she was insistent.

Now he stared so hard that everything dissolved and he had to give it up.

They say she has some kind of sight that others do not. Odysseus made a little joke about it that last day before he left—if you treat her right, he said, maybe she will find buried gold for you at Mykenai. Is it possible then? Has she really seen something that I do not?

Perhaps. But then when one considers her position, a captive far from home, indeed with no home at all anymore (and here he observed that the tunic of this last child of the last king of Troy was quite ragged), wouldn't it be tempting for one with such a reputation to try to take advantage of a situation, in other words to make something like this up in order to curry favor with me.

"Well, we shall see."

All the same I will wait a little with my signal. If there is anything, maybe it will yet reveal itself to me. Or she might see something further.

After all if she is right, I just don't want to walk blindly into whatever it is, do I?

— V —

But something *is* wrong there—Kassandra, shivering and hugging herself round. And to think how warm it is. Nevertheless, she kept her eyes fixed ahead.

What? There stand people on a beach. A cluster of them with a pinkness to it is apart from the rest. The pinkness is too large for one person, it appears. Perhaps it is his wife and another relative, like a daughter— And that, sad to say, is all I can deduce.

How can I convince him then that I know. For I do—the sense of it had come to her as things like this always did, except that it was not easy to explain.

It is a kind of clarity with a—a hole in it. That is, like looking up at the sky on a clear blue morning and seeing a black spot there.

Now that would make him laugh, wouldn't it; indeed no matter how he may feel about me. I had best not tell him.

And so it would be the same as always. For in all her life (and very old she felt) no one had ever believed the truths of this experience nor cared enough to try to understand its nature. No one. Ever. Certainly not Hektor or Paris or Deiphobos or any of her other brothers. Not even Uncle Antenor and Cousin Aineas, whose views about things

usually matched her own; nor Priam either, her only special
friend.

It was like being cursed. As Hektor put it once with
regard to me, he with those little eyes of his deep-set in his
paunchy cheeks—I am cursed with a mind in my female
body!

·

"Hah!" cry all the young serving men when they hear.
What a good trick Paris has played. And the bath girls, they
are full of oh's and ah's over Helen's jewelry and things.
"Why one day," a kennel boy confides—and isn't it odd,
the left side of his mouth curls up just like Paris'—"I too
will go a-raiding in Greece!" "Teeheehee!" crow all the old
white-beards sunning themselves behind the garrison house.

Little princess in her pretty flounced skirt, she cocks her
head this way, gold bracelets tinkling, tilts it that. Then—
"Sh-sh. No one must hear"—slips into the great hall and
sidles along the wall. Except that there is no need to be so
tiptoeish, for they are all busy talking.

So one, two, three, and there! She is up on the throne
beside her father and he is giving her head a little pat, his
hand a big hairy paw, and she is nuzzling against his king's
robe—hm good, the gold-roughness. Maybe it will be over
soon, their conference, and there will be time for us to take a
little walk together before dinner.

Meanwhile Cousin Aineas' skinny face is working—
"We ought to give her back." And Uncle Antenor's little
pointed beard is going like a dog's tail—"Yes, we should."
Upon which Paris, who is not laughing now—"She is not
yours to give." And Hektor's cheeks are sucked in a little
too—"I should say not." Then the vein in Cousin Aineas'
neck begins to throb—"That remains to be seen!" Uncle
Antenor's too—"This is a matter of state as well as phallus!" And then they are all quiet.

The way they act tickles her, and she is about to haha.

But her old father would not like it. So she closes her eyes and pretends that she is not there.

And then it happens or rather comes, and so very clear is it, what she sees, that—

But then—oh no!—it begins to go away again and— quick! Catch it! Before it—

She does. Then—"My father, Uncle and Cousin are right. Make Paris give the Greek woman back. It will only bring us great trouble if she stays."

"My father!"—Hektor, Paris.

"She is no fool"—he stroked her hair again.

"Then marry her off so she will make us some men who aren't fools"—Hektor.

"Har! Har!"—goes everyone.

"She is not ready for that yet"—smiling at them.

Again she—"The Greeks will come, my father."

"Enough, my child." Then to them all—"Here is my judgment. The situation belongs to a man. Paris is no longer a boy. Let him arrange it as he wishes."

"But the Greeks!"—Aineas, Antenor.

"Let them come"—Paris.

"I will give them a thing or two to remember us by!"— Hektor.

"Enough"—Priam, rising.

But no, he must not go yet! She jumps up. He must— She begins to quiver. "They will come, the Greeks, they will, my father. And when they do, they will kill all of you!"— her hand sweeping round.

Then she races past them.

To where?

Anywhere, to cry and cry.

All is lost this way, and they do not see it!

•

That was the first instance of the clarity, as she was to call the curious experience somewhat later in life. It came again a few months after this. By then, Priam having decided not to marry her off after all, she had been enrolled as a novice in the Athena temple (so that later when she was a priestess, he had explained to her privately in his chamber one night, she could "prophesy" to her heart's content without anyone's troubling her). Hearing that a Greek embassy had landed that morning, she had climbed up on the wall with everyone else (the whole city practically) to get a good look at them as they rode in. There was Menelaos severe in the eyes; Palamedes, the lean one on his right, seemed quite concerned too. As for Odysseus who was managing the reins, while his face was long also, he was a little—I did not know how—

And there it was again, and the truth it told this time was as important as the other, she had immediately realized, if in its way not more so. At least, she had felt, they ought to try to prevent that Odysseus from seeing where the weaknesses in the wall were. So late that night, after everyone around her was asleep, she had sneaked across the way to the palace and her father.

But strangely—and even today I am at a loss to understand—Priam already knew what she was going to say or seemed to, and it did not appear to matter much. "Hektor will take care of matters, my child," he had assured her. "Let us leave it all to him." And with this he had given her head a little tap as of old and bade her leave at once, lest she be discovered missing over there and her virgin vows be suspect.

The next time the clarity appeared was on the return of Odysseus and Menelaos, now from their camp at Aulis and with a new third one, Diomedes, big and bluff. But it happened that she could not go to her father right away as her bleeding-time, begun a few months before, had come that night and the pain was so bad for some reason that she could not leave her bed. So she had sent the new truth to him—how Diomedes was of the same mind as Odysseus—by a serving boy. All the same it had been too late to do any good, for after meeting with Priam and Hektor all day in vain, the three had immediately gone away again.

Feeling better the next morning, she had slipped over to the palace and happily found Priam alone.

He seemed very low, older somehow too. "Everyone wants a war, my child."

"But can nothing be done?"

He shrugged.

"What about Uncle Antenor and Cousin Aineas? Haven't they—?"

Now his shoulders fell.

And she? She went away with hers down too. It is done then. They will all die here, my father with them. And I? I will end as some miserable Greek's war prize.

After that there was no instance of the clarity, at least a major one, for a good long time, until everything was almost over. In the meanwhile, in the years that followed, she did as everyone else who was not directly involved in the hostilities—the women, the children, the old ones, eventually even the wounded, that is, those who could make the climb—and watched events unfold from above on the wall. She heard Hektor happy-shouting on the plain every day; saw those who jumped to obey him cut down, sometimes two-three at a time—their brothers, Antiphos, Troilos, and Mester; Antenor's best lifeblood, Antilochos and Akamas; Hektor's special friend, Pandaros; allies like Sarpedon of Lykia; and countless others. And then when his end came, Hektor's, how they all cried out up there around her. She too, for regardless of how he felt about her (and that had never changed; to the very end he had usually ignored her when she was in his presence), they were still of the same father and mother.

After he was gone, the command fell on Paris alone, who

had neither skill nor stomach for close fighting. Nor was Priam of any use anymore, being feeble with weak and watery eyes by then, like an old grandfather. And then when help ceased to come from the outside (the strangers, those horse-riding women and the black men, were the last), it was just a matter of time. Maybe they should have given the whole thing up then, sent Helen together with all of their gold out to them, the Greek-faces, and been done with it. She even suggested as much once. But no, Paris— or actually his lust—would not even consider it. As for Deiphobos, he took over after Paris not only with the men but in bed with Helen too, and he was another Hektor, maybe even stormier (he looked like him as well). Why he even spoke (this was after having seen Neoptolemos all smart in his father's war gear) of launching a new victorious campaign in which he would use friends of his, youths like himself, together with those not too severely wounded. But he never got the chance fortunately for him; he would have died disappointed.

On the day of the end she had sensed what was coming; that is, there was no need for the clarity to appear and tell her so. Still it had, and still she thought that maybe she could somehow do something.

•

She wears the silver-threaded tunic of the Athena high priestess now, and she can speak out if she wants to and does. But it appears to be useless, for though her father sits on his throne he neither sees nor hears anymore, or if he does, he no longer seems to grasp his perceptions. Nor are Antenor, old and failing himself, and Aineas, just plain weary of everything, of any help either; their eyes almost never leave the ground these days.

"Listen to her, she thinks she knows better than we"— Deiphobos to his friends. No one is hidden in the thing, he argues. After all how could there be? It is very hot in there and there is no air. Anyone trying it wouldn't have a chance of surviving, let alone creeping out and doing any harm.

Now a scout comes with a report of empty huts on the beach and the enemy ships all gone, and he brings with him one that he has found there, who has stayed behind on purpose—or so he claims, the serpent-face. Why? Well, just before they all left, Odysseus, his chief, whom he had served long and faithfully, flew into a rage with him over some trifle. And the horse, what was that for? Oh, Odysseus left it there as an offering to Athena for a safe voyage home.

Then one remembers—"Ah yes, Odysseus did worship Athena too, didn't he?"

And the rest—"Why so he did."

•

All the same she felt that she had to keep on trying. How could she not? Too much was at stake and first and foremost the lives of Deiphobos and the men. Where would everyone else be—the women, children, old ones, and Priam, Antenor, Aineas and herself—without them?

•

Try as they might, Deiphobos and his, the horse will not fit through the gate, and they have no choice but to break down part of the wall to make a passage for it.

"Listen"—she points as they are rolling it over the rubble.

But only she among those watching seems to hear the clang of metal inside.

Now it is closer, and—"There!"—the sound is more pronounced. Someone else perceives it and he speaks up. It is Laocoon, the high priest of Poseidon, and he is as they usually are, tall and sturdy with a voice full of authority.

Why not move a little of the wicker and straw aside and have a look in, he says; it won't do any harm.

"Yes, why not?"—others in agreement.

But Deiphobos is furious and absolutely will not hear of it. They have made the noise up, the two holy ones, and— "Why don't you both go back to your temples and prophesy there and leave the rest of us—soldiers, men—in peace. To enjoy our prize in peace!"

There is one last chance and she takes it. Grabbing a spear from a guard, she makes a deep thrust into the thing's flank. But curiously the point enters there easily and comes away clean.

"There, you see, that's how much she knows!"— Deiphobos. Whereupon he and the others give it a few more pushes and the horse is in.

"Hooray! Hooray!"—from seemingly the whole city. For everyone who could manage it, she realizes, has been watching the contest from the wall.

.

No one. Ever. Not any of them ever believed. Or understood . . . and now it will be the same with Agamemnon.

Only in all fairness to him he was interested enough to inquire further when I told him the "truth." So I should keep on trying to find out something more for him, shouldn't I? I am almost obliged to. Now what is wrong there?—examining the shore again.

Everything, however, was more or less the same as when she had looked a few moments before, except that the pinkness in the cluster did belong to two people she now knew for certain, and most likely they were women, but that did not seem to be of any real significance.

I need the clarity to come again. Yes, except that this time let it be a real clearness; that last one was scarcely a glimmer. There was little chance of that happening at the moment, however, as her head was too full of Troy to receive anything more just then. And so we shall probably have to wait and see, as he said.

That same day (she would never forget it) Deiphobos and his friends maneuvered the horse statue into the upper city and stationed it before her temple. Then that night—

.

Darkness with stars blinking through. Smoke, the smoke of victory hangs heavy in the air, biting the nostrils, clawing the throat.

Deiphobos could hardly have failed to invite her or she to refuse him, so she is there but has chosen to remain apart on a balcony. They are all gathered in the courtyard below her—Priam, laughing at he knows not what, holding on to Hekabe, who smiles as best she can; the young Polyxene, one of her sisters, who, while the odious Achilleus strove on the plain, saw only him from the wall and not as an enemy; Hektor's wife, Andromache, and their little son, Astyanax, both of them looking very solemn; Deiphobos himself and her other brothers with their wives and children; and of course Helen, who has not stopped with those eyes of hers, it seems, since first stepping from Paris' chariot.

Well, it will all be over in the morning, she thinks. Later, after they are all asleep, whoever is there in the horse will go sneaking down to the gate and open it for the rest who are hiding somewhere close by. Or not even that, the enemy will come through the breach in the wall. So. She turns away.

Down in the city the singing is loud and raucous, as it has been all evening, and everywhere—"*Pop-pop*"—hands seem to be clapping, and—"*Thwack-thwack*"—sticks beating out time on tables; and lyres are twanging and pipes screeching. Here and there an argument erupts with heated words flying back and forth and slaps or punches following;

once in a while flames leap up from a roof as the thatching of a house catches fire.

But isn't there a little too much brawling going on down there? In every house almost. And aren't there a few too many houses burning? On every street, it seems.

So, I was wrong. They are here now, I think.

Her eyes dart back to the courtyard to see if anyone else is aware of it yet. No, everything seems the same. Then the next moment—"*Boom!*"—the door has caved in and the whole place is swarming with the hateful ones, and Deiphobos and the other men are lying on the ground dead or dying (he has received a spear in the groin), and Hekabe dragging Priam, and the women and children are running round and round shrieking.

Soon Priam is also down, two with swords having yanked him loose from her and hacked him to his knees. My father! —she, not quite believing it all yet, still crouching low up there so as not to be seen. Oh!—suddenly feeling it and beginning to tremble. If only I can—

And she starts to crawl along the corridor, hoping to reach the stairs, which at length she does, then jumps up, scurries away, and gains the street and her temple. Flying past the horse there, now with a gaping hole in its side, she races in and slams and bars the door, and sinks to the floor gasping.

Maybe they will not find me here. Or if they do, let them kill me like you, my father. But this is not to be, she knows. I will be given to one of their leaders and he will carry me back across the sea with him. And she lies there starting from time to time when a shout or cry reaches her from outside.

Soon she hears a footfall, and then before she can think about it the door is down, and one of them, a common soldier, is there before her.

Instantly she is on her feet again and running, but to

where she has no idea—only away from him. Nor does she get very far. Having given chase almost at the same moment, he catches up and grabbing her by the hair sends her sprawling.

She lies there motionless, wondering what is next. Then it is suddenly quiet and she senses that something not good is about to happen and raises her eyes, not wanting to see really. He—his thighs are coming toward her, the phallus ready.

Oh my father, this too? Must I? This too?

"Yes, my child."

What? Is that he? Didn't I see them—

"We must all pay, my child."

I? Pay? Why? What for? What have I done? In fact— It is not just, my father.

"There is no justice in these matters, my child. Take it."

"Go ahead!"—Hektor Paunch-Cheeks.

"Who do you think you are anyway? Why should you alone among us escape unscathed?"—Paris Silver-Laugh.

"Go ahead and take it"—Deiphobos Boy-Face. "What difference can it make to you really?"

"No, I can't, I can't!"

Now he reaches her and drops to his knees, and she tries to squirm away—"No!"—and then when she fails to, lashes out at him with her fists.

He begins to wrench her legs apart. "I can't!"—clawing at his mouth, eyes. Then, the next moment, she feels a tearing into her down there. "No!" And there is a hot spurt. "I won't!"

Now he is on his feet again, she too somehow, and she is striking at him blindly. I don't want that in me (beginning to feel blood or both ooze down the inside of her thighs). "I don't!"

He gives her a shove with his shoulder and she falls.

"I don't!"—trying to get up.

Then with his foot—

.

No more! I have had enough. And now on the deck she wanted to move nearer to Agamemnon and stand close to him and feel his warmth, and somehow have him lean toward her (though as she had come to know him such a gesture was clearly too much to expect).

For strange as it might seem, and it was considering how during all those years on the wall she had despised his eyes and mouth most of all—

He is all I have now.

.

Sleeping. Waking. Stone, cold stone. Arms, thick ones, have lifted and are carrying her, and a man's voice is giving orders brusquely.

Soon she is set down again on something, and creaking it begins moving slowly forward with her. Her eyes blink open. She is lying in a cart with a Greek soldier managing the reins and it has just passed through the temple gate.

The city is finished, she sees, as they roll along. Visible everywhere are smoking grey shells of houses and charred bodies.

Once she hears a dog barking—ah, life. But then she observes that there are two or three or maybe more of them and they are fighting over—

Done. End.

A little further on, her driver makes the cart swerve to avoid something in the way, and she feels a pain down there and begins to remember—thighs coming toward her. At that moment a sound like a shout reaches her ears. And then there is another and another, and they seem to come from somewhere up ahead. Soon, with the wall before her, she spies a group of old people standing by it. Did those noises come from them?

Just then a Greek soldier descends the stairs and gets hold of one of them, a man, and begins spear-goading him back upwards. Above wait two others with spears. As the old one gains the top step, those two begin advancing toward him on either side. "Please! No! I don't want to yet!" But to no avail: they reach him and the poor creature has shot into the air and is tumbling down to his death below on the other side of the wall. As the cart moves through the gate and out onto the plain, she hears another meet the same fate and still others after that.

Then all at once it is quiet back there. Is that it? Is that all of them? She raises herself up a little and turns around. Apparently, for the loathsome ones are all alone now.

Gone then. Gone.

She is about to look away when suddenly something new up there catches her eye. The two soldiers have a large basket, like the ones used by the washerwomen of the palace to carry the dirty linen down to the river. They give it a heave and out fly five-six-seven things. They look like dolls, and at first she thinks they are but then realizes. Now the pair are taking the basket below, probably to get another load of the same.

All over. All gone.

She turns around and sinks back and closes her eyes. . . .

The camp is bustling when they reach it, everyone hurriedly sorting the contents of carts newly arrived from the city. On one of the piles amidst gold and silver plate lies a familiar robe.

"My father."

They wind in and around among the huts for a while, then come to a halt before one of them. "In there"—her driver.

She drags herself to her feet using the side of the cart and makes a little jump down. Flakelets of dried blood scatter from her—like tiny autumn leaves descending.

Inside she finds a sheepskin and eases herself onto it. And soon, her eyelids fluttering, she feels a nothingness or rather a blankness (for nothing implies something, does it not?). And this blankness begins to roll backward like a warm summer mist, until it has recrossed the plain and is home. Then it moves down along the coast past Mysia and Sidon to Egypt, billowing out there.

"Now I know everything," she says in the dream. "Therefore I can sleep."

But is this sleeping, this not being aware yet thinking? . . .

Someone is unhappy, a girl. And someone else, a man— no, there are two—they are not being very kind to her. A person should not listen when a man and a woman are alone together, or so she has been taught by her nursemaid and later her serving woman. But in this instance it is difficult not to; they are in the next hut.

"Let me be. Please let me be!"—the girl.

"Oh come on, we're not going to hurt you"—one of the men.

"No-o-o"—the other.

"Oh, please, no!"—she.

"Hold her!"

She screams.

Then after a few moments—"There. Your turn."

In a moment or two she screams again. Then there is silence and it seems to have a kind of finality to it.

"Think she's dead?"

"Don't know. I'll give her some wine."

"There. She moved. You can finish now if you like." . . .

Kassandra has just sat up and her hands have gone to her ears, but of course it is futile. If they don't stop it soon, I don't know what will be with me.

Then sensing something, she throws a glance toward the door and sees that he has come in, the detestable high-leader. Only she does not care who it is. "Please!"—pointing in that direction.

He seems to understand and goes out, and a few moments later it is quiet over there. He returns without a word and comes to stand before her, remaining there for some time.

Soon it occurs to her—I must belong to him, and he is here to—for the same thing. Well, why doesn't he then and get it over with?

Then he does something stranger yet; he turns around and leaves. Well, he'll be back, I'm sure.

Now she notices that his sword is lying by the door. He must have dropped it there just then, and this is also strange. Even so she goes to get it, brings it back and lies down again.

There is blood on the point she discovers, the girl's probably and—it is all for the best, I suppose. Then soon, handling it—maybe it would be for me too if I—

She begins to consider where the best place would be, the throat, the chest? And as she does so, her heart begins to race and head to whirl. To calm herself, prepare herself for it, she falls to studying one of the blade's sides. Depicted there is a grove of gold and silver papyri, and in their midst beside a stream full of silver fish a golden leopard is gorging itself on a silver duck.

Ah, Egypt, the shores of Egypt, so, so far away, yet so close. . . .

Presently there is a footfall near the door, and looking up, she sees that he is there again. As I said.

Only once more he just stands and stares. What is the matter with him? Why doesn't he begin? If for no other reason than to put an end to it, his eyes on her always, she—"Is—is anyone of mine—left?"

He proceeds to tell her: Hekabe, rather than go with Odysseus to whose lot she fell, chose to be sent over the wall with the other old ones; Polyxene at her request was sacrificed on the grave of Achilleus.

So.

He continues, and she listens, but vaguely now: Andromache is to follow Neoptolemos to Thessaly; Aineas has perhaps perished in the flames of his house with the rest of his family; Antenor and any of his still alive, if found, will not be harmed.

As I said. Finished.

Now all at once she feels—good! That is, somehow free, like—yes, like Egypt! And she begins to get warm and steamy all over like the marsh there, especially about the face. And there down there it begins to whisper (which when it has happened before she has always answered with a finger, this being permissible according to the previous high priestess). Well then, let it, that is, until he does what he pleases, or doesn't, and goes. At which point I will—

Except that now on looking up into his eyes, she suddenly understands what it is with him, and there down there it begins to call, issuing through her mouth—"Yes!" And then, the next moment, her arm is wound around his neck, and it has pulled his head down and forced his mouth on hers, and she has drawn his tongue from it, warm, hard, wet—I, the leopard! Where, oh where is it, the duck?— her hand seeking on him.

Ah, there—finding it. And she brings it into her. But then before it can, before she even has a chance to—the leopard is gone. It is gone! And he is trying to get up and go away again and leave her.

Oh no! I will not let him. No! Not until—and she grasps him with all of her might, holding him there. Soon she feels it once more, in there once more—and now it is for me. I, the leopard!

And she swaying, he, Troy is falling falling all over again. Until—

Wineblood!

And she, the duck—

.

Yes, he is all I have. . . .

But what is it? He had been saying something to her, and
she had failed to hear.

He repeated it having realized this—"What do you see
there now?"

"There?"

"Do you see anything further?"

She directed her gaze to the land again. Everything was
now plainly visible. That pinkness in the cluster on the side
did belong to two women. One was dressed very elab-
orately—that must be his wife. There was another in grey
by her—a servant probably. And behind them was the
other in pink—or is it red?—this one younger than they,
and beside her was another, younger yet, in white—his
daughters most likely. It seemed a little odd the way the
four of them sat there with their hands in their laps while
the rest of the throng was jumping up and down and flailing
the air. But then they were a royal party. So she—"No,
nothing."

Yes, he's all I have—and that was not inconsiderable
when one bore in mind that what they had done together on
that first day was repeated more or less in the same manner
on just about every one thereafter, that is, while they were
going along by Mysia and Lesbos after setting off for here.

There are also his shoulders, their bigness; yes, I like that
about him too. They seem so enduring; they most likely will
be sheltering as well.

Nor does it hurt that he is a high-king. Why he is probably just what under normal conditions Priam would have
wanted as a husband for me, everyone else, Hektor and
Paris, too.

And he still wants to know about my truth.

If only there were a way of bringing on the clarity again. Would it help if I stood so, loose-like, as I did when it happened before? She tried it. But there was nothing, or rather only a memory of that other time. Well, let it be for now; maybe I will do it again in a little.

So what is to be my fate when we are there on the land? He must know by now, my man. I only wish that he would tell me. She did not recall any captive women in her father's palace. Some there must have been to be sure, but try as she might she could not picture any. Of course there was Helen, but obviously because of Paris' longing she belonged to a special class of these, and Priam had acted accordingly, making available to him and her so large a suite of rooms that it virtually was a palace. And Helen was always free to come and go as she pleased, even (this was before the war naturally) outside the city if she cared to.

Anyway one thing is certain: I am not Helen, no, not in any respect. In fact if my face is anything like these (eyeing her hands, which were blackish), it cannot be too good to look at right now. The circumstances are different too: Sparta was standing when Paris took her from it. Also, who knows, she may have left of her own accord. That Menelaos was not much, as I recall.

On the other hand there is good reason to believe that he has some liking for me. At least he did not trade me off for another with one of his men while we were sailing along there in the beginning, which he could have, yes? Here she remembered how sometimes after they had done it and he was lying on his back all lazy-eyed, she would pass the time gazing down at him, and now and then she had even run a finger over the hard boniness of his cheeks and the smooth thinness of his lips. It never seemed to give him any pleasure, but then he never objected to it either.

It is possible then that he will establish me in some degree of comfort. But how? Where? They say that his palace is rather small compared to ours.

Wouldn't it be nice if there were a little house for me somewhere? It does not have to amount to much, just someplace where I can be by myself without anyone bothering me.

As for food and things like that, I can manage alone, I think. Or if not, at worst I would need a serving girl. Surely he would not begrudge me that; after all it would be only one.

Then maybe between attending to the affairs of his kingdom and resuming his life at home, he would be able to find a little time and come by and see me now and then, and it would be with us as before, a little. . . .

Now as the ship slid along, she swaying the while, it came. And so shaken was she by the new truth it brought that she could not help herself—"Your wife has someone! That is what is wrong! She has another man!"

He remained as he was, making no effort to respond.

Wondering, she looked toward him. Ah, what have I done!—for his eyes were strange and his jaws set. Where was my head? He probably had something with his wife and for all I know it was more than with me. Yes, I mean *that*, and remember, they have children.

Still what was I to do? He had to know. For if she has ridden down here to meet him like this (seeing, now that they were really close, how truly grand the woman looked in her different shades of pink—like Helen's sister, which she is, if I am not mistaken), her intention clearly is to conceal that she has someone else. And so the two of them may be up to something.

All the same (a sidelong glance showed that his face was unchanged) I have certainly not accomplished anything by telling him now and in this way.

So there is only one thing to do.

Except that I wish I knew. . . .

Still she did it—"I was only guessing about the man. But something *is* wrong."

This time she sensed him make some movement. Only on shifting her eyes to him again—worse! I have made it worse! Now the rest of his face—his cheeks—were rigid too.

"Whatever it is, if there is anything, I will see to it"—Agamemnon.

Yes, now he is really confused and angry as well—with me! And because of this when we arrive at his palace, he will turn me over to his chief serving woman and I will be lucky if I ever see him again even once. She and her minions will give me all sorts of chores to do that are beyond my strength, like carrying heavy cauldrons. And when I cannot, they will beat me; yes, they will treat me just like a slave, and there will be no one to intervene on my behalf.

Worse yet, thanks to my stupidity, he will probably not give a care now about what is secretly going on under his nose, and his wife and her man will have a chance to do him some real harm if they have a mind to. . . .

The ships had all begun to drive forward on his signal and his men had taken up their oars. Now some of those on the shore—boys, old ones, even women—were charging into the water and soon, in a matter of moments, the men would be throwing the cables to them.

"Hail, Agamemnon!"—the crowd.

Is there anything that I can do?

No, not really.

Only hope that he will not be all that foolish.

Home! Home!

— *VI* —

As I thought, she was just trying to influence me to do something for her—Agamemnon, waiting while the ship was being drawn along. And I will, but as I said, later. For the land-jolt was coming—there!—and now they were beginning to wind the cable round a tree and it was time to get down.

He jumped outward bracing himself for pain, which there was, a twinge when his toes hit the ground. But all in all it was quite bearable. For he was home, feeling the good solid earth beneath his soles. Yes, Hera, home at last.

But why is it so quiet suddenly? A moment before all the people there had been gladly shouting. Now no sound whatsoever came from them and their eyes seemed to be fastened on something behind him.

What is it? A quiver went through him. He turned his head.

Ah, it was the men. Most of them were down on the land too, he saw, the rest of the fleet having been hauled in— and oh Hera, no wonder they are all staring so. The men were a far from pleasant sight, as a matter ·of fact pretty shabby-looking.

Why I must be like that too. He peered down at himself. So I am. And here and there beneath the dirt he noticed the skin was sort of pale purple. Nor was his tunic greyish originally, if he remembered correctly, and it seemed to be torn in a few places.

Still what is there to get so wrought up about? All it needs is a little— And he could almost feel the warmish steam curling up and into his nostrils, the strong girl's hands working over his chest, back, with a stiff sponge, knocking him from side to side in their zeal, then done and dry, another experienced woman's hands pressing the cool sweet oil into his hide, especially the back of the neck there. However, all that will probably have to wait until tomorrow, as I do not think there will be time today.

"Welcome home, sir"—a soft manly voice from close by his side.

Now what? Who can it be? I am not expecting anyone here to meet me—and again he began to shake a little. Nevertheless, he chose once more to turn and look.

But of course, the captain. How could I have forgotten. "Thank you, captain"—grasping his outstretched hand.

This seemed to have a thawing effect on everyone. "Look, there is my Aristides!"—a woman, pointing. "Where?"—others, her friends. "Patrarchos! My Patrarchos is back!"—a second. "Is he? Show me!"—those near her. And the next moment all flew together—from the shore, the ship—and it was cheery-noisy once more.

"Is everything all right here, captain?"—above the din. "Yes, sir."

"My wife?" (He looked her way. She had risen. He nodded and she gave him an eye-blink back.)

"She was in a bad way for a time, sir, you know, when she returned. But she is fine now."

I like that fancy pink she has on. She looks like Helen

in it—that is, as he remembered Helen at Sparta those years ago. Which should not be surprising, should it, hah?

The girls, they are big. But I do not see the boy with them. "And my son? Is he here?"

"No, sir. He is in Phokis with your friend Strophios. He was getting restless, you know how it is. So the queen and I thought it would be a good idea to send him there."

"And is he all right?"

"As far as we know."

There was a lot of loud talking, especially toward the rear, it seemed. Now he heard coming from there somewhere—

Aie, Aie, Aie
Aie, Aie, Aie

And off to the left he made out smoke rising. Oh yes, the thanksgiving; I almost forgot it again. He began moving toward the wisps, the captain by his side, those in the way —the men, their loving women—shifting a little to let them through.

So, Strophios. He and Strophios had grown up together in part, for Atreus and Strophios' father had been special friends and according to custom Strophios had spent some of his boyhood with them at Mykenai. As I recall it, though not much to look at, he was quite an expert with his weapons after Atreus got finished with him, and I can remember the two of us then hunting together with much good feeling.

So now my Orestes is with him, learning of him, and is friends, I trust, with his son—Pylades, I think the name is. "You have done well, captain. It will not be forgotten."

"Thank you, sir."

As they reached the neatly piled stones of the altar, two temple girls brought the heifer up, all shining white and gold, and the senior priestess, black-and-gold lady, gave him a nice smile for his little bow of the head. So now we are going to make the thanksgiving. I still find it hard to believe—we are here.

Two other girls stepped up dance-like, one with a gold basket, the other a gold basin.

Aie, Aie, Aie
Aie, Aie, Aie

And he began. "Oh Hera, accept of this, our offering of thanks, for our safe return." Now he took a pinch of barley from the one and threw it on the fire, now sprinkled a little water from the other, and then receiving the gold knife from the senior priestess, sawed off some hairs from the animal's head and added them.

Aie, Aie, Aie
Aie, Aie, Aie

But what next, what shall I say now? And it was very quiet too, everyone having shushed one another in order to hear.

Well? The sweat began to form a little under his arms. What did Atreus say on these occasions? He took a deep breath.

Then before anyone really noticed it, somehow the words came. "Thank you, Hera, for letting our eyes feast once more on the golden ramparts of Mykenai and our feet revisit silver-shining Korinth and—" Good, I will go on like this.

But now all at once there was a new problem. It was as if a huge wave had crashed nearby and sent a whole lot of spray flying at his face and some of the salt had gotten into his throat. He was going to—

But no (he took another breath), I must not. They can, let them, but not me.

And who knows how it would have ended had he not just then heard it. Indeed there was no mistaking it. The sob had come from one of them there. And that did it. Yes, let them. Then as the rest of the names fell from his lips—Kleonai of the great walls, flowering Araithryea, horse-pasturing Genoessa, sea-swept Aigion, Orneai, Hyperesia, Pellene—there was another sob and another and another. Good, only let it be them. Them!

The holy woman handed him the gold club. This part I don't relish, but what choice do I have?

Well, it will be over in a moment. He raised it to his shoulder, ready.

Just then the animal lowed.

"Ooh, the cow!"—someone.

"It's crying!"—another.

Now it flicked its tail and tried to back away, and the girls worked hard to control it.

"It's a bad sign!"—someone else.

Everyone murmured.

He let the club fall to his side and—please! His eyes ran here and there, searching. Unless something is done the thanksgiving will be ruined, and then so will everything else most likely.

"Ah!"—coming from everyone.

He looked back. The captain, good man, had sprung forward and grabbed the creature's horns and forced its head down, and some of the men, seeing this, had jumped up to help him hold on. Oh thank you, Hera, thank you. He brought the club up again. All I have to do now is come down with it, and that will be that.

And he would have. Only now something—I do not know what it is—but I can't. And with this sweat covered him all over, and the sinking feeling—that feeling again!—

came on inside. Eh, this is bad—his eyes began to hunt for something again. Very bad—as somehow they found his wife staring at him.

But I must do it. If I don't, what will they all think?

All right—making an effort and breathing heavily. I will, or I will try. But after this—

He let the club sag behind him over his shoulder, leaning with it, then snapped forward.

"Hooray!"—the crowd.

The clubhead had landed right on the crown.

The men dragged the animal up, its forelegs having folded, and he took the gold knife again and pricked the neck-vein.

Aie, Aie, Aie
Aie, Aie, Aie

No more—trying not to watch as a girl squatted to catch the bloodfall in the basin.

Aie, Aie, Aie
Aie, Aie, Aie

Never again!—turning away as the thing's eyes became glazed and his own began to burn once more.

Aie, Aie, Aie
Aie, Aie, Aie

It is over—blinking hard. I have done it—he heard them begin to strip down the carcass and get it ready for spitting.

Yes, and now I can go home. . . .

What's happened? He seemed to have lost track of things for a moment. What's going on? He looked at the altar again.

The roasting done, the senior priestess was heading in his direction with one of the smoking sticks.

Partake, my son, her look urged him as she halted before him. The meat, all shining and blackish, was inviting too.

Yes, Hera, I will. He grasped the spit.

He bit off a piece. Hot, it is hot!—rolling it round in his mouth. Still he managed to chew and swallow it. And that did it; yes, the searing drove his tears away—once and for all.

Enough—giving it back to her with a wave of the hand. She moved on to the captain with it.

"Now me! Me!"—everyone, reaching, as the girls followed with others.

Yes, a good pain, that is all one needs sometimes. . . .

"My son?" The priestess was there again, now with a gold goblet.

He took it and held it high. Everyone, mouths greasy, became quiet again. "Once more we thank you, Hera. May your kindly eyes watch over us and your caring arms succor us always." Then he tossed the dark red fluid onto the fire.

It shot up bright yellow.

"Good!"—someone.

"It is good!"—they all seemed to agree.

The priestess went away and returned in a moment with the goblet full again. Now is the best part. He took a swallow, a long one—ah, grapes of home. Then another—fine, fine heat—in his chest, cheeks, and passed it back to her.

She went and refilled it once more and brought it to the captain.

"Me next!"—again everyone, reaching out, as the girls began to come round with cups.

So it is over, I have managed it (the ground shifting a little under him—like the sea, hah). "Any news of the others?"—to the captain as they drew aside. "Is my brother home yet?"

"No, sir." (Nor anyone else from hereabouts with the exception of Nestor, it turned out.)

"And—Odysseus?"

"We have heard nothing."

Where can they all be? Is my old comrade still raiding somewhere?

They had been moving toward her, his wife. Now almost there, the captain—"I have brought three carts, sir. Will that be enough?"

"For what?"

"The things from Troy, sir."

He sort of smiled. "There is nothing, captain. We lost it all in the sea."

But why does he look like that?—observing him suddenly look odd. I did not make the storm or steer the ships toward Maleia!

They were before her now. "My queen"—with lowered eyes.

"Agamemnon"—almost in a whisper.

But has she nothing else to say? I am home! So, she is still angry with me.

"Welcome home, my father"—Elektra.

"My father, welcome"—the other.

He nodded. Fine, these two, well-kept, well-dressed, the red, the white. The boy will be the same, I am certain. Well, I will have to set it to rights with the mother somehow.

His chariot drew up—ah, real gold—and the soldier driver, a young one, hopped down and ran to hold the bridle. He, to the captain before turning to climb in—"Be sure to announce that we will have games this afternoon. Choose some things from the treasury for the prizes. Then after that there will be a banquet for my helmsmen and stewards; announce that too."

"Yes, sir."

Now for home. He put his hands on the chariot's side. At last—curiously remembering his pallet, good old sheepskin, back there in his hut at Troy. Must be tired. Well, maybe I can get a little sleep before the games. He began to haul himself up.

But just then a hand touched his shoulder. "My father, I would like to speak with you."

He swung around. It was his older, and she had a kind of hurt look in her eyes. Has she missed her father then? So. "Yes, my child." Ah, if only she could—

"Why not wait until later, my princess"—the captain now between them. "There is plenty of time. Your father has just arrived."

Good fellow, stole the words right out of my mouth. "Yes, later, my child"—giving her a little smile. Right now let me—

"But my father—"

Ah, she is disappointed. Still—"I shall see you first thing in the morning, my child, I promise. Yes, you will come before all other business."

He climbed in and took the reins. And I will too, even though I already know what she wants. What else would a girl of her age be after? Only I will not give her an answer at once; I must have a chance to think it over first. For it wouldn't do to marry her just to anyone, would it?

Finally!—the captain had handed his wife up beside him. It will be good to get out of here if only to see just land again. He gave the horse a flick.

But what is this? The horse had moved sideways. Something was in its way. He peered over its head.

Yes, there was something, like a small pile of old clothes.

"What is it?"—his limbs beginning to tremble again for some reason as the captain went over to have a look.

"It's nothing, sir, just an old one."

"What is he doing there?" Have I—!

"He claims to have seen your ships before anyone else."

Yes? So he wants something. He saw and now he wants a reward.

Meanwhile the heaplet had arisen, a man. "It is true, oh king"—coming up to him. "I was the first, oh king."

Ah, the face all withered, the tears trickling down it. "Well then, good man, we must reward you." Only he did not have anything, he remembered, no, by Hera, not even a ring to pull off. "Take care of it, will you?"—to the captain.

"Yes, sir."

The old eyes brightened; grey-brown they were like the cheeks. "Thank you, oh king! Thank you!"

He nodded, then turned his attention again to the horse, which could go now. They began rolling forward.

"Har! Har!"—someone behind him, it sounded like one of his men.

He gave a look round. Whatever it was, maybe his jaws could go *Har* a little too. After all, of grief I have had more than my share.

A small group of them with their women were gazing up at his ship and his captive there on deck. His lips came together—I forgot all about her. She was still in the prow where they had been standing but he could not see her face. It was covered over by her hands. Ah, the poor thing, unhappy because I am leaving her.

What shall I do? The chariot was moving. I still don't know, but tomorrow after I am finished with my child I will take care of this one and I will think of how soon. If nothing else, I will have her brought to the palace and put in the servant's quarters.

As for now—he caught the captain's eye. "That too"— with a jerk of his head in her direction.

.

"But, sir—" Only the effort was in vain, for his king was gone.

And that was not all. No, the captain had another question for him. What am I to give this old one here? I do not carry things around with me like a lord to hand out to people. At any moment now he is going to start nagging at me, and then what am I going to do?

"Captain, what about my reward?"

There, you see, already. "In time, good man, in time."

Then there is Elektra over there behind me, all ready to go home and try to make mischief again. "Calm yourself, my princess. We will be leaving shortly"—over his shoulder. How am I going to manage with her?

And even more urgent than this old one and the princess as a matter of fact, where is my woman? For no sooner had the ships come in and he had gone over to greet the king than, lo, when next he looked around during the thanksgiving she was no longer there by the queen, indeed had vanished. So where?—craning his neck.

Oh, before I forget (seeing that some of the returned ones were beginning to leave now)—"Games next! Games everyone!"

Maybe I just missed her and her husband. They could have found one another as soon as he landed and gone off at once before the ceremony began.

"Games! Remember the games!"

Yes, that must be it—as he eyed one in particular, who was with his woman. And where have they run to?—noting that they held one another closely round. They are deep in some trees somewhere. What are they doing there? She is on her back so, and he—he is sliding his phallus in and out of her in his fine steward's way.

Or maybe he is lying there and she is—with her mouth. He sauntered over to the water.

But what am I thinking?—dipping his feet in. If he has

turned up in the same condition as these others, it will take more than one of her baths and a fresh tunic to make him as he was before. Why he might not be able to do it at all and for some time to come. So all I have to do is wait. For after being with him like that for a while, a couple of days at the most, she is sure to seek me out again.

He wheeled around. The place was all but empty now and the few stragglers left were going too: a one-legged man with two women holding him up on either side, his wife and his sister from the looks of them; another with nasty running sores all over him, but with only a stick to lean on.

Of course if he is like one of these, he may never do it again. In that case she and I—it will be as always.

Then he saw her. She was moving toward him just as if she had appeared from out of nowhere. And she was all by herself.

Her eyes were red-rimmed and her mouth opened and closed, but no sound issued from it. At last and so low that he saw rather than heard it—"Washed overboard."

Is it possible? Who would ever have thought? And now he wanted to—

Yes, why not? This once let us forget about everyone else and their problems and go in among the trees somewhere ourselves. There in the cool of the shade they would lie down together, he with his mouth on hers, and soon with his hand finding the right place between the hairs and going up and down, but lightly, it would grow all oozy there, and he would do it to her neatly—until she makes not a sigh but a shriek, yes, a great shriek, so that all the birds there go jumping into the sky!

Eh, I can carve a roast up too if I really want to.

But those tears that she has been shedding, what is the reason for them? Are they for me, because she is glad to have me, her steady man, back again or, rather, sad over the loss of the near-stranger? And if it is as I suspect, will this grief of hers be so profound that she cannot—

And how long will it last?

"Will I see you later?"—as tonelessly as he could manage it, still with chest thumping.

A moment passed. Then—"Yes." And the corners of her mouth turned up a little too.

Oh! Now he wanted just to put a few fingers on her, that was enough really. Anywhere, even only on the nose, which I can do here now if I care to. It doesn't make any difference anymore if anyone sees, does it?

No, it still might displease her for some reason. So I had better save it along with everything else for later. Instead let me see to these problems here and right away—for there were a lot of things waiting to be done at home, he just then recollected.

First, as to the captive (she was no longer visible, having disappeared within the ship as soon as the king had left), since he did not tell me otherwise let us assume that he wanted her to stay in there for tonight, not such a bad idea. (Indeed he had already given it some thought on the road this morning and then again while standing and waiting here). If the king and queen can spend this night alone together—well, there is a possibility that— Well, why not? After all hasn't she by making herself look so nice shown that she is willing to try it again with him? Now if he is like-minded—and why shouldn't he be, she being the injured party—given the chance, it might be with them as before, when she was having the children.

The only problem is tomorrow. What will be then, when he hears? That Elektra!

But maybe I can get to him first and try to explain. What?

I can tell him what a really bad state the queen was in at first, and how we feared for the worst, my woman and I—which isn't far from the truth, yes? . . .

Eh, it needs more thinking about, but not now. I must return to these other problems. Maybe later, when there is time, I or my woman will yet come up with something. . . .

While the captive's not being in the palace that night seemed desirable, it was not all that simple a matter for her to remain where she was. Not long before a returned one or his woman had thrown a rock or something at her and hit her, and now there was a gang of boys hiding behind some bushes by the ship. Unless something is done, as soon as my back is turned they will all be for climbing up there to stick their little things into her.

All right, how is this for a beginning? He bent over and scooped up some pebbles. "You there, I see you! Get out of there! Go home! Now!" He let fly with them at the bushes.

The boys yelled and took to their heels.

Very good. The only thing is they might come back again after I am gone. I could leave one of the men here, I suppose. But I have a feeling that I am going to need every one that I can lay my hands on later at home. So?

He whirled around. "You!"—to the old watchman.

"Yes, sir. Yes, captain."

"You will stay here and keep watch over the woman there, do you hear?"

"But captain, my—"

"Never mind that. You do it, or I'll—" His hand went to his dagger.

"Yes, captain! Yes, sir!"—backing away.

Next! Next was Elektra. This is not going to be easy; in fact it may very well prove to be impossible. For the only solution, he now saw, at least for that day, was to get her home slowly. But while he had been busy with those other matters, the girl had gone and gotten into her chariot. (It

was under some trees with the carts a little distance away.)
And now with her sister there beside her she was ready to
leave in a hurry.

Why not give it a try? What do I have to lose? He hurried over. "My princess, your father is expecting the stewardess and me home right away. Would you mind letting
us—"

"No!"

"My princess, he will be very annoyed with us if—"

"I don't care." And "*Whack!*"—she was gone.

Let her then. I tried. There is nothing further I can do.

But now came an unexpected piece of good luck. (Honestly it was enough to make a person want to take Hera a
little more seriously.) Just as the chariot was about to disappear around a bend one of its wheels got caught in something!

Only with Elektra continuing to beat the horse that
struggled in vain to obey, it came off!

Instantly he was there and shoring the vehicle up with his
back. "Come down, please—quickly, princesses!"

They did so, and he let it go with a crash.

Elektra was visibly shaken, the little one too, ah. So looking everything over (it was nothing, the dropped wheel was
only stuck between some rocks)—"Princess, the chariot is
finished." At the same time he motioned for one of the
men, an old-timer, to bring his cart.

It jounced up and he handed them both in.

"Now go carefully, do you hear?"

"Yes, sir."

They lumbered away. Good, at that pace it will be night-
fall at least before they are there.

He waited, his fingers tingling, and at length when they
were a fairish distance off beckoned for the other two he
had there, both of them sturdy youngsters, to come and
help pry the thing loose.

Then this done and the chariot upright again, he shed and chucked his cuirass in the back and drawing his woman up beside him he was off.

But gently, hah.

.

Yes, I am really home—Agamemnon, on the plain, the horse trotting briskly along. And with a new strength.

Or is it the wine?

Maybe a little, I admit it. But only a tiny bit. Most of it is from you, Hera, and again I am grateful, truly.

And now— But how fresh everything seems—recognizing apples and pears and almonds and figs and plums and pomegranates green-ripening on either hand and everywhere the rich red-brown land succoring them.

And it is mine, I almost forgot. I don't know why, but I did—mine to enjoy for the rest of my life. Why I can stop off anywhere along the way here and pick up some of the earth and let it run through my fingers if I please. Mine.

Look!—as they passed two fluffy white goats under a sparkling green tree with the copper-red earth all around them. Peace, it is peace! I will remember it always. . . .

A day like this is for going up to the pine forest—was, rather. It's too warm now; face, chest—sticky-itchy. I'll go tomorrow then. Yes, I'll take my spear in hand and— Oh but I can throw one, straight to the mark almost every time. Even Achilleus admitted as much when he would not let me enter the contest at his precious Patroklos' funeral games, claiming that it was because I had more than enough prizes already. Anyway I'll rise up very early, while it is still dark out, and jump in my chariot and—

Why there must be game everywhere! You can almost smell it. Sh-sh. Walk only on your toes and don't breathe, for there is a boar in that brake over there, and he is as big as a—

Eh, I have been dreaming. Not good. Too many things to think about now. One day soon I will go up there again. But as for now, first I must arrange to have Orestes brought back; yes, he must be sent for at once. Should have told the captain straight off. But no harm done, I will as soon as I see him again.

Orestes, does he look like Atreus, I wonder? But perhaps that is too much to expect, and no matter.

If he and Pylades have become special friends, as I imagine they have, then Pylades' son can come and grow up here with my grandson. That will be nice.

Except that before that can happen, Orestes must have a wife, mustn't he, hah?

Let me see. . . . The obvious choice is Menelaos' Hermione, especially if Helen makes no other children (that is, a son) for him, which seems likely in view of her age. That way the two kingdoms can be united, as they would have been to begin with had I—

Oh where is he, my little brother? Still on the sea and contending with it as I was? Not storm-tossed, I hope. Hera, bring him home, will you. For I have something to say, must try to explain a few things to him.

But I ought not to forget my girls. They must be attended to also. One will have to go to Pylades, I suppose. There is no way of avoiding it: one favor begets another, that is the way of the world.

Will he be content with the younger? If so, then the elder can marry—ah—Nestor's eldest, Peisastratos, that is, if the old one ever speaks to me again. If not, then when he is dead and buried, which cannot be too long from now, I should think.

Then if Elektra chances to have a daughter and it is an only child, why it could be married to Orestes' son. And then, hah, Mykenai, Sparta, Pylos. . . .

Meanwhile what will be with this one here beside me? I said that I would try to make it up with her. Why not now?

"It's all the same"—he, nodding at everything around them. "Nothing has changed."

She did not answer and he sensed that she remained as she had been, with her eyes dead.

Shall I try again?

Yes, but with something different.

"I am going to have Orestes brought home."

She blinked a little.

Is that all? Let her sulk then if she wants to. I tried.

Somehow it was warmer now, indeed truly stifling, the sun, though not directly overhead anymore, seeming like a great drop of hot smoking oil. And now all at once he was drowsy. So he leaned against the chariot's side—hard gold—and lowered his eyes.

.

Iphigenia is small and tender—like my captive—so in her short tunic with her hair loose and feet bare she seems even younger than she is. But if there is any pain as he leads her along she does not show it. Only when they reach the altar and then her eyes (wet black they are) say—oh do not do this, my father, I am your child.

Still he signs for her to kneel, which she does.

The diviner makes a slit at the top of her tunic with his knife and tears it down to her waist. Everyone—Nestor and the rest—murmurs at the loveliness.

Now the man pushes her head onto the stone and gives her father the blade, saying quietly—once will be enough.

He puts the point on the place, only just then—"No, my child!"—her mother is there, and I'm glad, he says to himself.

But then Odysseus stops her and someone has a cart

brought up and she is put in it, and—"Get it out of here!"
—he hears himself shouting.

Then he returns to his little one.

Tears are running down her cheeks and her limbs are quivering now. No matter. He does it, he must—"To the gods."

The diviner grasps the knife and makes the blood come more. "To the gods!"

"The gods!"—everyone, as the eyes begin to fade.

.

Drip-drop, wine gone. Head empty, dull, except for a little pricking above the right eye.

Have I been asleep? Apparently, for somehow they had managed to pass through the town without his being aware of it, and now the citadel gate was directly before him.

His eyes sought the stone triangle above it and found in it the familiar column flanked by two rampant lions with raging golden heads, Atreus' emblem. Yes, everything the same.

"Hail, Agamemnon!"—men, overhead on the bastion.

As I said, everything.

He reined in the horse and an old soldier latched onto it. Then stepping to the ground, he would have gone round to the other side to help her. But before he could make a move even, she had jumped down by herself and run away.

Eh, she has cause—as he watched her rush up the ramp, the stairs. Still, will there ever be peace between us?—as she disappeared within the gate above.

He started upward himself, slowly. Someday, I suppose; it can't last forever. That is, unless—he lurched a little. Unless there is something more to her anger.

Like a man! Another man? As my captive said?

No, what am I thinking? She would never have dared. Or else, supposing she did, imagining that she was getting even with me, who was there for her to do it with? Everyone was with me, yes?

Then even if she did manage to find someone, from somewhere else—Strophios and his people stayed at home, for instance—the captain, he would never have allowed it.

Unless— Now he nearly fell.

No, that is impossible. The man has always been loyal to me and served me well. Besides why would he have?

Why does anyone?

Foolish! With me returning one day or another, it would just not have been worth his while, no matter what he got out of it.

Still (on the stairs now, with cheeks taut) maybe I ought to— Perhaps the man should be retired and another put in his place, say, one of those just returned with me.

Of course I will compensate him generously for everything that he has done. "Why I will treat him like my own son." Give him a parcel of land to farm; he will like that, I think. "Who wouldn't?" And a woman to go with it, that too probably.

"The stewardess is a good choice"—now that her husband is no more. Past childbearing, though, if I am not mistaken, but as I remember it, strong, dependable, hardworking. Yes, she will suit him fine.

Finally, with head buzzing, he was at the gate.

And then my captive, why she can be—

.

How I hate, no, loathe him—Klytaimnestra, on reaching her chamber. There are really no words to describe my feelings about him, their depth. You wait! I will get you, I will fix you! You will see!

She began taking long strides up and down. But after a few turns like that—the day is far from over. "And there is the night too." She settled into one of the chairs by the hearth.

Oh how happy I was to see those ships of his come in as they did, without a sail among them, and his precious men and him in rags. And when it turned out that his hoard of Troy-things was at the bottom of the sea, I could have howled with joy. There is some justice in this world—his world!—after all. To kill a child, his own child.

And that! Imagine it, no sooner has he arrived than there he is doing it again. Yes, I know that it was an animal. Still—

Then after in the chariot—to think of it—behaving as if nothing had happened, even saying as much. Why I could have done it to him right then and there had I been strong enough, and with just my bare hands on his throat. And he knew that I was feeling like that too, telling me then that he was going to send for Orestes.

He deserves far worse than a knife in the back. I have a good mind to go to him at this very moment (he is probably in his chamber) and tie him down somehow (which means that I would have to bring along a thong as well as a knife) and— What?

This is what: take his phallus and put the knife to it, and then as I watch the pain spread across his face when he realizes what is going to be, say—"This is what you made the child with, this is what you hurt me with again and again, and it is because of this that the people all follow and serve you right or wrong." And with this draw the blade over it and—"Now look at it!"—fling it in his face.

But too far, I have gone too far—nursing her left side as she felt a stab there like the pain of this morning. It has all been for nothing too. I would never do anything like that, no, not even if I had a chance to.

As if I were not weary enough already—recalling that she had spent almost the whole day down at the beach.

And in that heat—her eyes feeling heavy just at the thought of it. Almost as soon as they had arrived, the sweat had begun to run on her, and everywhere, under her arms, between her breasts, down the inside of her thighs. So big the drops had been that she had imagined tears. Yes, it was a little like crying. I don't know what I would have done without the stewardess' fan and willing arm.

Also, with everyone suffering in the same way how it had reeked there after a while. Worse yet, the women had made a little place for themselves in some bushes (she herself had to go and squat there a number of times), and as the day wore on that had come to sour the air too.

Nor did matters improve any when the ships finally landed. Then she had to stand through that sad horrible scene.

Meanwhile the stewardess had disappeared, and then had come the final blow: Elektra had begun. I still don't understand. Doesn't she realize that if he learns he will not hesitate to kill me? Does my daughter really want to see me dead? Lucky for me the captain was there; I couldn't have done anything. I was too numb. . . .

Now arms weighty, legs—it would be nice to lie down again for a while.

She rose and slipped off everything but the blouse and after carefully draping the jacket and skirt over the chair stretched out on the bed. If I lie very still, my hair will be all right too. If not, the stewardess can fix it later when she comes to get me for the games.

In the chariot with him and in the midst of her fury twice something odd had happened. The first time was as she caught a glimpse of the citadel in the distance. With the sun slanting that way, suddenly it had seemed all golden but bloody—yes, it looked like a lump of gold with blood on it, this place. And a voice inside her had said—a bad thing is going to occur there; do not go. Then later, near the gate, with the bastion and wall looming on either side—so thick they are too—she had grown almost icy cold. At the same time a dread had arisen in her that when the doors slid open something monstrous and slimy would be waiting there. And the voice inside her was more insistent this time—run away! Something terrible is about to happen here.

And it will soon. She yawned, then closed her eyes.

And the plan? Is it still all right?

Her eyes slowly opened again. As far as I can tell. But he looks so—weak. He might not want to.

That will be better; in fact it will make it easier all around, won't it? All that I have to do then is get him to sit in one of those chairs there, a simple enough matter if I am going to tell him something. Then at some point or other I will go and find the knife here in the bed and—

The good thing about it is that his back will be to me.

Even so I must be quick about it and prepared for any eventuality, like not striking right the first time.

What about Elektra? Will she try to tell him again before morning?

She might, but it won't make any difference. I think I can assume he meant it when he said that he would not see her until then. There is one thing about him I know for certain: he always does what he says he is going to. So I have until then, time enough.

And his captive, what will the captain do with her?

I don't know, and it is of no consequence. At any event I must not think about it right now or anything else for that matter, only of making sure that he gets here.

There was a knock at the door.

That is the stewardess, I expect. "Yes?"

"My queen?"

It is. "Just a moment"—she went to slip everything on again.

— VII —

"In the dark, my queen?"—the stewardess, bringing a small torch to light a lamp. For so it was there, though outside some time remained before the sun went down.

This was her third stop since returning from the beach. First she had led the captain into the pantry, and they had partaken of some cheese and bread and wine together (when she had given it as her opinion that Agamemnon, on his learning everything, would not be too hard on them, his servants, their part in it having been without much choice really). Then she had gone up to her lord and when he had refused to take a bath—though I don't know why, there was time enough—fetched a basin to sponge him down a little at least. Now the lamp flickering, torch out, she was here to find out what she could do for his wife.

"How is it?"—Klytaimnestra, turning around to let her see.

She examined it all—the hair, the face, the dress—as a stewardess should. "It's not bad, my queen, truly."

"I tried to be careful."

"No real harm done." Then the stewardess set to work brushing some more pink on the mouth and a little more white under the eyes, combed out and rewound one of the ringlets and restored order with a few fingers to the spit-curls.

"How is it now?"

"Good, my queen." Nevertheless, the stewardess patted down some flounces and smoothed the jacket in the back.

"Do you have the rosewater about you?"

"Yes, my queen"—finding it in her basket and passing it to her.

"I shall need another bath later, I think"—as she dabbed her neck, arms.

"All right." Then—"Ready, my queen?" And almost seizing the flask from her, she steered her out the door.

For there are ever so many things to see to here—as she set the pace for the two of them down the corridor. And what with those serving girls of hers not having returned, nor would they this day anymore most likely—I don't know how I am going to manage.

It's the banquet I'm worried about most—they were step-step-stepping down the stairs now. I suppose I can make do with some of the boys from the garrison. Also if I have a few of them search diligently in the town, maybe they can find some old ones or children to come up here and give me a hand.

Still what I really need is a good right one—now they were on the ramp. Would my man be willing to help out, I wonder? I should think so since it means pleasing the king.

But he doesn't know anything, how to make the slices nice, treat the wine.

Eh, he will learn as we go along. . . .

They had left the citadel behind them. Down the road a little way the captain was waiting for them, anxious and with good cause. There within the gate the stands were full and the king was already on his platform.

He gave her a relieved look, then began leading the

queen across the field toward their master. She followed their progress, at the same time taking in all the men there. Just imagine if my husband had turned up like one of these. Why whatever would I have done? For if it had been bad when they landed, now (white seemed to be the only color there except for the ruddiness of their faces and arms) it was even worse—

"They have clean tunics on top of their filth!"

As for my captain (gazing at him still walking with the queen and remembering his look at the beach when she told him the sad news), well, he will do better at everything from now on, or at least he will try.

.

"Here she is!"—someone. "Here she comes!"—others. "Hooray! Hooray!"

How loud they are—Klytaimnestra, nevertheless making little nods to either side as she went along. Have they been drinking or what? It certainly looks that way—noticing some very shiny eyes and a wineskin here and there among them. It is all right with me as long as they don't fight. Yes, let them be noisy but peaceful. Blood I will have more than enough of later on.

He looks better, my husband—seeing as they were nearing the platform that like everyone else he wore fresh white. His face seemed lighter too.

Apparently he is not going to speak to me—he had not looked her way and did not now. Probably he is irritated because I did not say anything to him in the chariot, that is, did not agree that everything is beautifully the same and show my heartfelt appreciation at his intention of having his boy brought home.

"There you are, my queen"—the captain, supporting her under the arm for the step up. She turned and took her place beside the king.

"Let's begin!"—the men. "Yes, yes, begin!"

By all means, let's get it over with.

The captain motioned for them to be quiet. "The first event is the footrace"—Agamemnon. "Who will compete?"

No one came and everyone began muttering.

"There are good prizes"—he again, as the captain held up two talents of gold, a gold tray, and a silver goblet.

Still no one appeared and the hum of voices grew louder.

Why what is the matter with his heroes?—she.

But of course: they are upset because they have lost their Troy treasure and now their substance is no more than what it was when they left, maybe less; whereas this is obviously not the case with him.

I wonder just how angry they are. Is it possible that with some more wine they could become really hot and fall on him and save me the trouble? I might if I were they under such circumstances.

Is that a good idea? Do I want them to kill him like that?

It is tempting, but no, I think not. For then they might not stop at that but go on and do the same to me—or worse. So, no thank you. Keep on, all of you, with your grumbling if you like, but stay where you are. I'll do my own dirty work, if you please.

"Will no one try it?"

"Hooray!" A short one with a deep broad chest had come down, and another, a tall lean one, followed him. The first tried some bursts back and forth—"Hooray! Hooray!"—while the other kicked up his knees and shook out his legs—"Har!"

"Anyone else?"

One more, a loinclothed youth with long dark hair, joined them—"Hey, a boy!"

"Begin, captain."

The three stepped up to the starting line, a row of stones set in the ground, and hunched themselves over. Then the captain's arm shot up and off they went, down, down, toward the turnpost, feet pounding.

Will the young one win, I wonder? I hope so, though it will probably upset these here even more.

She gave a sideways glance to see if her husband were following it. He was, but stonily, it seemed. Too bad. With the runners doubling back now, their arms striving, legs churning, and everyone cheering, had he ventured to speak at this point, in all likelihood in the heat of the moment she would have responded.

So don't, it's all the same to me really.

The three were almost at the finish line now, the youth, his hair flying, slightly in the lead. "Come on, Atymnios, catch him!"—the whole place, to the big-chested one who was just behind him. That is, except for a little group in the stand to her right who urged the youth on—"Don't stop, Polybos, keep going!"

Suddenly Atymnios put on some speed—"Hooray!"— but then tripped and fell—"Oh!"—leaving Polybos to come in alone.

So he did it, he won.

The youth walked over to the platform and knelt before them. "You ran well, my boy"—he beside her, as the captain handed him the gold wedges.

"Thank you, my king"—his chest heaving.

But he is not all that young, this Polybos, she decided, as he went on his way; just looks it because he is short. I wouldn't be surprised if he turned out to be my Orestes' age.

"Well done, Atymnios, a good man, Atymnios!"—everyone, as he scrambled up and went to collect his prize.

Yes, he is easily that—her eyes following Polybos as he climbed back up to his place. But unlike my son this one here does not hate his mother; yes, of that I am sure. He cannot, not with a look like that. For now among his friends, who were all glad-whispering and fondly patting his shoulder, he was gazing down at the field almost dreamily.

"Next is jumping"—Agamemnon, the third prize having been disposed of amidst more hooray's and well-done's to the tall thin one.

"There are good prizes for this one too"—no one again had presented himself and the captain proceeded to display them as before. "Anyone?"—vaguely, the field still empty. There was murmuring once more.

Apparently not this time. Now what will he do? Something foolish, I hope.

No, she was wrong. Polybos had come down again, and with him was another, smaller youth who resembled him, a brother perhaps.

"Who else?"

But that was all. Fine with me—and she watched as the two sprang up and down to get ready, their hair tossing and falling.

"All right, begin."

They moved back as far as they could, almost to the platform. Then Polybos sprinted forward and as he reached the line flew into the air with his legs kicking. The other followed, aping his movements, but landed considerably behind him.

She used to be fond of someone like Polybos, in her youth, she recalled. He had worked in her father's stables. And for some reason, whether because of his eyes, which were dark and tapered at the corners like this one's, or how he carried himself, in the same way, like a fully grown man, he had meant more to her than any of the others she had taken a fancy to in those days, and the fascination— savored with the rest in the privacy of her chamber—had lasted longer. . . .

"Good boys"—her husband, the two of them having made another try with the same result.

"Thank you, my king"—they together, kneeling.

"Let's have some wrestling now!"—someone, as they went away with their prizes, a gold cup and a silver dish.

"Yes, wrestling, wrestling!"—a bunch of others.

"All right"—he. "Who will do it?"

"Hooray! Hooray!"—as two of theirs hopped down and faced one another in a circle of stones.

It was a little comical for they were both about the same size, and what with their bushy hair and darkish skin (they wore only loincloths) it was truly difficult to tell them apart; and when each at the captain's signal began using the crooks of his arms on the other's neck, it was well-nigh impossible. However, no one seemed to be tickled by it except her. Instead there was "Get hold of him, Lykon!" "Strangle him, Menon!"

Will that be? A lot I care. Still it is an ugly way to end. She decided to turn her head away should it begin to look as if that were going to happen.

But this was not to be, fortunately for her—them too, I suppose. Having fallen on top of one another and rolled over several times locked in each other's arms, suddenly they split apart, this Lykon and Menon, and—"Hahaha-haha!"

"Come, you men, enough"—he, lightly.

Eh, go on and smile. You will not be amused for long.

The two dragged one another up and lurched over to the platform. Then as they staggered away, with a tripod and a cauldron—"Heeheeheeheehee!"—from them and everyone.

"Stone throwing is next"—he. "Someone?" Then when no one came and it grew noisy again—"Captain, will you?"

Fine, that is how I want it to be. Only let him have more uneasy moments like this.

The captain entered the circle with a stone. It was the size of a boarhound's head but from the ease with which he carried it, seemed to weigh little more than a pebble.

"Now who will try his skill against the captain here?"

"Har! Har! Har!"—a gang to the left, an unusual contestant evidently making his way down through their ranks. A boy around ten years old walked onto the field.

"Sir?"—the captain.

"Proceed, captain."

He hefted the stone in either hand and pawed the ground with his feet, then wound himself up and let it go.

"Good, man, good!"—he, the thing having spun clear across the field and almost into the stands there.

The captain went and retrieved it and presented it to his opponent. But just as this small one was about to give it a heave—with both hands, and knees bent—he scooped him up and whirled round with him as if to send him flying.

"Hahahahaha!"—everyone, including Agamemnon.

Enjoy yourselves, yes, now. None of you will in the morning, believe me—especially one of you.

"Now boxing!"—someone. The captain had set the child down and sent him away with a little ivory-handled knife. "Let's having boxing!"

Another of theirs, a large one, bigger even than the captain, strode out to the circle, grinning.

"Is there a challenger for him?"—he.

"You fight him!"—someone. "Har! Har!"—others. He showed his teeth in response.

I dare you! I dare you to do it!

"Well?"—he.

"Feed the captain to him!"—someone else.

He nodded to the captain to go ahead, and the man would have, only—

Oh, no!—Polybos was there.

"Good, he's a good one!"—many.

No!

The captain bound the leather pads onto the youth's hands and he began dancing around and poking the air.

"Hooray for Polybos!"—his friends. The big man, who did not need the captain's assistance, having managed the thongs with his teeth, knocked his fists against his palms, testing them. "Go and get him, Iloneos!"—everyone else. Isn't there anything that one can do?

They stepped inside the circle, and instantly Polybos began slugging away as hard and fast as he could. The whole place rose to its feet—"Come on, Iloneos, finish him!"

Please, someone! She turned to her husband. But his eyes and mouth were as they had been before—so it does not matter to him. And the captain?—shifting her gaze to him, on the other side of the circle. But his face also seemed impassive, and his hands were behind his back—so he doesn't really care either, I guess.

Isn't anyone going to try to stop it?

Apparently not, for Polybos was still swinging with all his might and everyone still urged the other on. Then, the sun coming to touch the arena on its way down, they all looked like bleeding copper, and somehow she knew from this that no one would.

Soon Polybos' pace began to slacken. At the same time Iloneos, who had done nothing of note up to now except shoulder-shove the youth to provoke him, began holding off himself. So that a moment came when both of them stood stock still. Then suddenly one of Iloneos' arms shot out, and—"*Crack!*"—down dropped Polybos holding his face.

"Nice work, you gave it to him, the upstart!"—some, a large chorus agreeing, as Iloneos strutted over to the platform. He held his prize high, a gold tankard with men handling bulls embossed all over it. "Hooray!"—everyone, on seeing it.

Then they all began filing out.

But isn't anyone going to see if the boy is all right?—he hadn't stirred from the ground.

Obviously not, for the place was still emptying and very fast.

How can they be so cruel, and to one of their own, and a young one too? Can they really just leave him like that?

She looked toward Agamemnon again. But—I might have known—he had already gone himself, and she made out his back on the other side of the field.

And his comrades, the boy's?—her eyes going to their stand. Ah, they too had left, even the other jumper. They will be back of course as soon as it is quiet here. They only ran away out of fright.

Or if they don't for some reason, why (noting that the boy was sitting now) he will manage on his own, I imagine.

Still I can't understand why— And then suddenly she realized that she was trembling and in earnest. I didn't think that anything could ever affect me like this again, no, not after her, my Iphigenia.

How shall I go on?—her head hanging all at once.

"My queen?"

It was the captain. He had put the remaining prizes in a basket—and now he wants to take me back up to the palace with him.

"Yes"—giving him her hand for the step down. The light was about to disappear too, she saw.

Then, as they walked along—but of course!—the answer came.

.

It is a real wintry night, the first since Aigisthos has arrived. Outside where we have just been to look, a chill wind blows and the sky is full of dark shadows on the move, marching. Now within the great hall the stewardess has tendered us warmish wine in cups and soft curly lambskins for our shoulders, and we huddle close to the hearth where she has a fine blaze going.

Of a sudden it occurs to me—it will be over soon. Yes, one not too distant day my husband will be sailing back here and if somehow Aigisthos and I succeed in surviving his wrath together or alone, sooner or later but all too soon another enemy, an invincible one, will arise. I cannot help thinking—death, that is when one does not see or hear or feel anymore, one is nothing. And when they put you in the ground, you are even less than that, being then unperceivable.

How gloomy I am, I tell myself, then realize that there is good reason for it. My bleeding-time is coming and I always have thoughts like these just before then.

All the same I cannot dispel this particular one. How does a person knowing that someday soon she or he will be no more—what do they do with the time left?

Maybe he has an idea. So—"Do you"—it is difficult to begin—"do you want something?"

He grins, mistaking my meaning, deliberately, I suspect.

But I—"No, you know."

His eyes lose their playfulness; indeed he is frowning. "No, nothing." And while looking my way, he no longer seems to see me. He has returned to the past.

It is all over and done with, I want to tell him. Forget it, forget about it. Or if you must leave me like this, let it at least be with a thought to saving us from the first catastrophe.

"Nothing? Have you no plans? No dreams?"

"No. My father—"

There, you see.

"No expectations?"

He grins, but not as before. "We were to capture the citadel, my father and I, if you remember. Then he would have been the ruler here (or so he led me to believe), and I after him."

"Well, it wasn't much of an expectation anyway, was it?"

"It was as the world goes, his and your husband's."

"But since then, now? What are your expectations now?"

"As I said, nothing."

"Nothing at all?"

"Moments then." And when I don't understand—"To savor each as fully as I can for as long as I can."

I am about to say something stupid, like what kind of an expectation is that anyway, doesn't everyone sooner or later arrive at such a conclusion? But just then the stewardess and a girl come in with wood for the fire (it had burned down the while), and I wait for them to finish.

Soon they have it as it was—no, better. It is a lush red with tiny golden lights, and on the walls around us shadows are going up and down like happy-leaping hounds. After they have gone, I slide my hand over to his to tell him that this is just such a moment. At once he returns my pressure —yes, it is.

"Of course you mean only the good moments"—I, pursuing it. "What about the rest?"

"No, the others as well, the bad and the good."

"Even growing old?"

"It is difficult but—"

"Even dying?"

"—yes, though naturally one prefers the good ones."

How is it possible, I wonder? How can a person savor them all almost equally like that?

I consider for a time. Then I recall a dream I had. It was just after my return from Aulis and prior to my man's arrival here. After reviewing it in detail—yes, I understand, I have all along really. And I relate it to him.

Something terrible happened here, like an earthquake, and with the palace on fire and full of smoke, I found it impossible to descend by any of the stairways and so had no choice but to move upward toward the watchtower, where I finally ended. But there I found myself no better off really, for the floor, weakened by the shock, seemed on the point of collapsing.

At first I didn't know what to do and wrung my hands. "Oh won't someone somewhere come and help me?" This was foolish of course, for everyone else was either dead or busy, and rightly so, saving his own skin. Then after a few moments, when no one appeared, I began to see the situation for what it was and realized that I could delay the cave-in by keeping my weight from being concentrated in a particular spot, that is, by walking around, which I began to do.

And as I did so, though under no illusions as to my prospects, understanding that sooner or later the wood and stuff under me was bound to give way, if not of itself then when I became tired and could not move anymore, I grew calm and began taking pleasure each time one of my feet came down before me.

"Yes, that is what I meant"—he.

•

"Look, the queen!"—the men. "Here she comes!"

Here is everyone waiting for me again—as she preceded the captain in.

The great hall looked different with so many there. Tables had been squeezed into it every which way and five or six men crowded on each. But—the smell! How they stink, all of them—as she wove her way toward a little space before the throne where Agamemnon sat alone with an empty chair beside him.

This time his eyes measured her approach, and there was a grave, almost sad look in them. So, what they did down there, his heroes, had an effect on him after all. I'm glad, it's about time that something did. All the same it's a little late now. I truly don't care anymore.

"Hooray!" Some of the young men of the garrison had issued from the pantry when she sat down.

But can the stewardess be serious?—seeing them with gold basins and pitchers and dainty linen cloths. Why these "heroes," they will—

And they did. "Look, I'm a Trojan!"—one, who had grabbed away a basin and stuck it on his head. "Wheee-eeeee!"—others, who had overturned pitchers on their neighbors. "Yahahahaha!"—still others, who were just plain drinking the warmish water. "Oh, he's so pretty!"—a few, having gotten hold of one of the young men and pulled his tunic up.

The rest had taken to their heels either back through the pantry door or out the other.

So much for niceties with the likes of these. What's next? Ah.

Some pale-mouthed women were coming out with steaming gold platters, and trailing them was a toothless one-eyed nanny hugging a stack of baskets to her bosom. "Hooray, the meat!" Two more young men followed uneasily, each with a load of gold plates. "Hooray, the boys!"

This bunch will fare no better than the other, I'm afraid.

And so it turned out. Laughter—as hands snatched at chunks of meat and pieces of bread, then—"Har! Har!"—at that which held them. Whereupon the women and the old one fled, and the youngsters set their burdens down anywhere and dashed after them.

The platters moved briskly along the tables, yanked this way and that amidst—"Oik! Yoik! Yoik!"—belches and—"Flub-flub-flub!"—farts.

She lowered her eyes and tried hard not to listen. As with everything else, sooner or later this too will have an end.

But this was not to be yet. Just then the stewardess appeared, her face all flushed, and behind her trotted the captain with a krater and two small twin boys with their heads shaved bearing bloated skins and a tray of gold cups. "Hooray, the wine!"

While she, busy woman, saw to the mixing, her man at a word from her went into the pantry again and emerged a moment later with something for the king and queen to eat and drink.

"Thank you, captain"—she, as he set the plate and goblet before her.

The meat looked a little mangled and the bread spongy, but when she took a bite of the one—it's pretty good, whatever it is, lamb, I think. And the other was not bad either, especially after she had moistened the whole thing with a few drops of wine.

She was about to repeat the procedure—starving—but by now the boys had finished passing round the cups, and— "Hach! Pach!"—there was a lot of sputtering and choking and even retching and—

No more! She gave her plate a push. . . .

You (looking sharply at them), you with your loud deep voices who carry on so—you do not know what manhood is. Why my Aigisthos, most likely he would not seem like much to you, but for me he is all in all, strength and caring too.

Ah, his shoulders, hard-knotty they are. His arms the same and thick. And his hands, I kiss them.

My tongue runs down along their knobby veins

Ah!

When he walks, it is always jauntily. I am particularly fond of the back of his head then, especially where the hair tapers and the neck begins to curve.

You should see him when he makes his water. He always leaves the door open a little when he does, so I know. I think he wants me to watch him. His body tilts way back as far as it can go, and his hands rest so on his hips.

And do you know something—I think it would surprise you—I did not like it with him at first. Oh, it was all right, pleasurable, if you know what I mean—do you? But there was something wrong. Have you any idea what that was? He did it without trying; it was effortless. And because of that it seemed as if he were with just anyone. But then I realized that this was not so, that he really did want me and me alone. Don't ask me how, it just happens with people after a while. But even the best of you would not understand this, would you?

What am I saying? The best of you would be the last to.

Every so often now when we do it, he draws his phallus out to the very end and holds it there, making me yearn to recontain it, then all at once goes in again all the way so that we meet once more, completely.

Would even that have any meaning for you?

One time when I asked him to, he made his juices stream across my breasts, and I licked a little of it and made a face, and he laughed.

Now sometimes after— But it is really sweet almost. . . .

"How about a song?"—someone. The boys had refilled the cups. "Yes, let's have a song!"—others. "Is there no harper here?" "Yes, a harper, bring us a harper!"—the tables began to rumble, the floor echo them.

The captain went out and led in an old blind one in a brownish tunic clutching a rude wooden—it looked like a lyre. "My lord and lady"—at a cue from his guide in passing and in a surprisingly mellow voice. Then some made room for him nearby, everyone shushed one another, and "*plink-plink*"—

> *Say, oh muse, how all-powerful Agamemnon*
> *Held himself in battle, high-chief, among the host*

Everyone began to say something to his neighbor.

But what is the problem?—the old fellow had ceased at this.

"Sing about the games!"—a shout.

So that's it. But what will be?—for he did not know the games, he was whining back.

"That's all right, we'll teach you!"—a chorus. Upon which three or four jumped up to sit by him and began talking together.

I can just imagine how their song will come out. Yes, first it will tell of the footrace most likely and how Atymnios would have won it handily, the hero, had his old Troy wound not acted up and forced him to give over the advantage to Polybos, an untried one. Then it will go on to relate —let me see—how Lykon and Menon could not bear to strive against one another in the wrestling, such good Troy friends were they; whereupon Agamemnon, wise leader, had presented them each with a valuable prize. And then they will bray about young Polybos—who would dare omit it!—and how he, his arrogance over his prowess knowing no bounds, had sought to clobber everyone's favorite in the ring, only to—

"Har! Har! Har!"—those with the sightless one.

Yes, that is how it will go, their song, and it looks as if it will be ready before long.

"Har! Har! Har!"—the loudest of that bunch, he with burning cheeks and a kind of yellowish beard somehow making her think of Odysseus in her father's great hall those years ago.

Enough, I have had enough, of them and everything. She rose. But before I go—

She leaned toward him and touched his arm. "A few words with you in a while." At the same time her other hand covered the knife she had been using and brought it down unobserved to her side.

"Yes—if you wish." He looked as if he had been sleeping.

Even so he has spoken. So now we can get this thing over with—as she began to move toward the door.

And when it is, let there be—no more blood!

Or ugly nastiness either, no matter what I agreed to about savoring moments with Aigisthos—with a glare at them all on going out.

.

I have it! I did it! (*In her room with the door shut, flaunting the knife.*)

Only will he come?

Of course he will; why shouldn't he?

I forgot to say the part about Orestes.

Eh, he will anyway. He said that he would, and he will. He probably thinks that I want to make it up, and since he was trying to do just that before in the chariot—he will come.

But he looks so bad, worse even than then, worn out. He may fully intend to but then fall fast asleep down there.

Oh, there is little likelihood of that happening, I expect, not with all that carrying on.

What if the captain sees him nodding and decides to help him up to his chamber? What will be then?

Little likelihood of that too. With that bunch angry like that and just beginning to drink, the man wouldn't dare leave, not even for a moment. No, when the time is right— soon—Agamemnon will rouse himself and come here, believe me. And then— (*Brandishing the knife.*)

Meaning that, as I said, after we have sat here for a while (*She takes one of the chairs by the hearth.*), I will get up and go over to the bed (*She does so slowly.*), giving some reason of course. Then finding the knife there where I will have hidden it (*Putting it down on the bed and picking it up again.*), I will—(*She turns toward the chair.*)

But isn't it going to be difficult doing it from the back like that?

Not at all. I will come down over his head in this way. (*Sweeping the air with both hands locked on the handle.*) All right, only I think I should begin a little higher—there, for instance. (*Raising it.*) Yes, that is better, except that perhaps my arms should go up with it more slowly and I should bring it down fast—like this. (*She goes through the sweep once more.*) Perfect.

But where should I aim for on him?

The throat is best, I suppose.

Yes. . . .

And now I must hide it and quickly. (*She turns around and slips the knife in among the covers, then returns to the chair and sits. A moment later there is a knock at the door.*)

Just in time, for either it is he—

·

"My queen?"

Or else she, the stewardess—it was. "Yes?"

"Is everything all right, my queen? Do you need anything?"

She got up and went to the door and stood there without opening it. "No. Fine. Everything is fine."

"Would you like me to help you undress?"

"No. I will stay as I am for the time being."

·

(*Remaining there.*) What will she think when it is all over? The captain too? They will not be pleased, I suppose.

Eh, who cares.

No, that is not so, I do. But that is not the problem, and there is one, I think. I can feel it: something is there somewhere in a corner of my mind sort of scratching at it. And to tell the truth it has been there all day. Now what is it?

(After a while.) Ah yes. I am not sure that when the time comes and my hands descend with the knife I will be able to do the rest of it, stick it in his throat or anywhere else. Yes, after all this. Why? It has nothing to do with him really; it's just that ever since Iphigenia, in fact even before that, as far back as I can remember, I have never liked the idea of someone or something dying, that is, like some people I know, the captain, for instance, Aigisthos too, who really seem to relish it sometimes.

Yet I dine on meat every day, have even looked on, and unflinchingly, while the thing was being slaughtered for that purpose, and just yesterday I shared Aigisthos' delight over his catch.

Yes, it is a contradiction.

Still if I do not go ahead with it my husband will learn in the morning and— So I have no choice, do I? I must at least try.

But will I be able to forget it afterward, the knife going down through the air and meeting and piercing flesh, the scream as it does so, blood flowing, groans and the death twitch, and all of this my doing? I think so. I may even be able to remember those moments calmly, though I will surely never savor them. For afterward I will have Aigisthos and he me. . . .

(She returns to the chair.) If only my man were here. How foolish of me to insist on his leaving. He could have gone down to his turn-off and hidden there somewhere until he saw us ride past, then doubled back and sneaked in through one of the sally ports, and waited. With my husband fatigued as he is, why as soon as we drove through the gate— But there is no use thinking about it. He did not do that and he is not here; only I—I alone.

Which is no different from how I have been most of my life.

Yet I am, and I must do this thing by myself.

But I have taken actions before in that way, though what precisely I cannot remember just now. One might say that I have been preparing for it, in training, all my life.

Yes, but unlike those other actions, I find this one very distasteful to say the least.

They say that it can be very gratifying to feel that everything depends on one's doing something by oneself.

Just the same I wish that Aigisthos were here. Only he is not, and so I must do it alone. Yes, this or die....

Supposing when the time comes I really cannot, what then?

I don't know. I could turn the knife on myself. If nothing else it would save me the agony of waiting for a possibly worse fate in the morning.

Yes, but would I?

Perhaps, perhaps not.

If I do, what will be with Aigisthos when he hears?

He will be very sad, I imagine. He might, blaming himself that he gave in and left me here—he might even—

No, I would not want that.

•

"My queen?"

But she is still there. What does she want now?—rising and going to the door again. "Yes?"

"Should I come back later, my queen?"

"I—no; it will be all right. I will manage by myself."

"Well then goodnight, my queen."

How composed she seems. Have things turned out to her satisfaction then? I did not see her husband down at the beach or, come to think of it, in the great hall either. Has something happened to him?

She opened the door. "Your—did he—?"

Gone: the answer.

"I'm sorry. Goodnight."

So, they have one another all to themselves and for good now, she and the captain.

•

(*She closes the door and returns to the chair.*) There is another problem, and this is also something I did not foresee. My husband has changed; he does not seem to be the same person who sailed away from here ten years ago, at least as far as I can tell, not having known him very well then. Yes, I don't remember ever seeing him with his eyes the way they were down there in the great hall, and I think that there was something else in them besides weariness—a kind of moroseness, a somberness.

But why is this a problem?

I'm not sure.

Do you feel sorry for him?

It is possible.

Come, come, do you or don't you?

All right, I do—a little.

The degree does not matter, you do.

So, so what.

(*After a little.*) Perhaps—it may just be that since he is not as he was—perhaps if I were to talk to him, he would be—reasonable.

(*Another pause.*) Perhaps. What would I say? I could not tell him about Aigisthos and me, could I?

Of course not.

Well then?

(*Again she considers.*) Why not (though naturally I would have to be very very careful when bringing it up) say that I would not be unreceptive to the idea of leaving here so that he could make his captive his queen. I would be content to go, I'd add, wherever he thought best. The details, what to do about Elektra in the morning (one would think that she would be satisfied when she heard and keep quiet) and how I would subsequently meet Aigisthos and so on, I could work out once he agreed. The question is will he? Is he capable of being *that* reasonable?

I really don't know. But there is only one way to find out for certain, isn't there?

All right, it's settled then, I will try it.

(*What sounds like "Har! Har!" and "Hooray!" comes from below.*) The heroes must have their song, or maybe it is over and they are teaching their harper another, this one, now that I am gone, about some nice little rape or a juicy seduction or a pretty piece of incest. For next to war and games that is what they enjoy hearing about most, I should imagine.

(*Now something like wood is being smashed down there, and there is a lot of shouting and at least once a scream.*) They must be breaking one another's heads. Excellent. Maybe they will include his as well while they are at it, which is quite all right with me now, being safely out of the way.

But if they don't, I will talk to him.

And if that doesn't work— Let us see.

— *VIII* —

Home, I am home—Agamemnon, on his throne, to which he had slipped on her leaving, the goblet (refilled more than once by the captain) heavy in his hand. And a cheery time it is, just as in the days of old, I believe. "Harper, give us a song about Atreus, will you?"

But the plinker did not hear. No one had. There is too much—too noisy here. "Quiet!"

That did not help either; it was even louder now. "A song" about Atreus, eh—sinking in the seat.

Then one day soon, when I am rested up, I will take a little ride over there to the temple and get hold of Thyestes' son; I don't know how, but I will. Orestes can come with me if he likes. He can bring his Pylades along if that suits him; it is perfectly all right with me.

Then when he is mine, I'll do as I please with him. And that will be the end of them, our enemies, once and for all. Imagine it, hiding the body in the pantry like that, like some dirt a child has made—that temple boy.

"Harper, please, sing about Atreus!"

"No, we want the war!"—someone. "Yes, do the war now!"—others.

The old one began—

Say, muse

"That's right; say, Hera, oh Hera." No, no, I must not do that, or else everyone will think that Agamemnon is stupid with wine, which—heh-heh—he is a little, but no one must know.

how wide-powerful Agamemnon

That I am.

                                   slew
All of the best warriors of the Trojan race

And that I did and will anyone else too who gets in my way!

First he drove on Bienor, himself a shepherd,
Thrusting the spear straight in his face as he lunged
So the tip passed through helm and head; and the brain

"No more of that, give us the games again!"—someone. "No, we are tired of the games!" "The games!"—others, with the first. "The war!"—more. "The games!"—still others, their fists rising. "Never mind them! The war!"—the rest, beginning to shake theirs.

Eh, time to go—pushing himself up with the armrests. Now where is the captain?—looking round with narrowed eyes. Ah—spying him by the pantry door mixing more wine. "Take care of everything."

"I will, sir."

Yes, a good man. He stepped carefully, it being wine-slippery there. Bodies—my poor men—were sprawled in the way too. It will be a pity to lose him, that captain of mine, but it cannot be helped.

He reached the courtyard without mishap. Now to bed—toward the stairs with a yawn.

No, first I must stop in there—pausing. What does she want anyway?—slowly beginning to climb. All the way home she did not even look at me and went off in a huff when I was about to do something nice. Now suddenly there is something on her mind that cannot wait until morning.

Well, whatever it is, I must try to be agreeable—having gained the top step.

"It will be for your sake, my son."

.

This time the knock was a strange one so it had to be he. She went to the door and opened it. They stood there for some moments, she with her eyes down, assuming that his were too.

How odd this seems, she reflected, but under the circumstances it is not so at all when one recalls that this is the first time we have ever been alone together like this—to talk.

At length she gave a nod and he brushed past her and went and took one of the chairs. She followed him to the other.

Her eyes sought the hearth, and keeping them there, she fell to admiring the fire, which was somehow rather pretty.

It is like little pink fingers there.

But soon—do you know I am beginning to think that it is a bit too pretty. For now it seemed as if the fingers were poking and beckoning, which reminded her of—I can't think what. Except that one could conjure up all sorts of pleasant but ultimately distressing events occurring beside it, like a young bridegroom leading his bride to the bed and there ensuing what the old serving women at her father's palace used to refer to whisperingly as "nuptial bliss" and the next morning and forever after "domestic harmony." No, I don't fancy this fire anymore.

Well then, begin.

But how? You know, I didn't give any thought to that.

So? Do it, come up with something now.

She glanced his way. He had been gazing at the pretty fingers too, it seemed; was doing so still. Then she noticed that his mouth was relaxed, cheeks as well, and eyes soft as if he were also savoring it.

No, that must not be. He must never—never savor anything! Enjoy a certain amount of peace perhaps, but no, not that! . . .

"Why did you kill her?"

He turned to face her but avoided her eyes. "The child?"

"Of course the child, who else but the child?"

"I— It has been a long— They wanted it, the others, the other leaders."

"But you were their chief."

"They insisted. They wanted it as a token of union. It is the way of men at war."

"Men? War? To kill a child for that? Wouldn't an animal have done as well?"

"I tried." His chin went down.

There, that is how I want it. Yes, you be sad like that, and then maybe I can find it in my heart to feel sorry for you.

But it is not over!

"Tell me"—she had begun to quiver. "Why couldn't it have been your brother's child? After all you were going to Troy to get the mother back, weren't you?"

She waited, half-expecting a response, but then when none was forthcoming—"I know, you don't have to tell me. We had several, they only one, so the loss of a child and a girl at that would not have made as much of a difference to us. Isn't that it? Isn't that the way you all reasoned it?"

"I—" His chin sank even further, almost to his chest.

"There is another thing, I have another question for you.

Why did you choose that particular child? Granted that it could not have been the boy; he was your son and heir—why did you not use one of the other girls? Why her?"

"They—the others—said that she was the most beautiful thing in all of Greece."

"They? They said? But they never laid eyes on her, only you and your brother and your friend Odysseus, whom you sent to get her with that—that story about the marriage!" And now had the knife been in her hand, she would have hack-hack-hacked at him—his head.

He rose—"There is no talking to you"—and began toward the door.

She jumped up and rushed after him. "No, you must not go! I am not finished yet!"

He turned round—he was on the threshold—face drawn, eyes lost. "What do you want me to do?"

"Do? Do?" She whirled to the bed and put her hand there. "Do to yourself with this"—offering the knife to him —"as you did to her, that's what!"

He smiled.

Oh, the thin lips!

.

(*Watching him go from the doorway, the knife dangling from her hand.*) Why did I do that? What is the matter with me? What happened then—the child—does not make any difference anymore, only Aigisthos and I, the possibility of our having a life together. So why? And to have shown him the knife like that. Who knows what he is thinking now—and going to do.

But I'm forgetting about his fatigue, and I suspect that he had a drink or two down there after I left. I got a whiff of something like wine now and then while we were talking just now. I can also count on his arrogance (which one never loses no matter how one changes in other respects, yes?). So she had a knife, he is saying to himself, and it was hidden in the bed. Well, what could she have accomplished with it against my superior strength? No, my guess is that he went straight to his chamber and will remain there.

On the other hand he will not be falling asleep so fast either, for I have given him something to think about, perhaps as no one ever has before. Yes, he will probably sit there for a while and mull it all over, what I have said and done, and eventually maybe even make some sense out of it.

One thing is certain then: I am going to have to consider the next step to be taken very carefully now.

(*She begins toward her chair.*) No (*Stops.*), there is nothing to consider really, I have no choice. I must go to him at once.

And do?

(*Instead she goes and sits.*) I will point out and convince him that it is impossible for us to get along anymore—hah —after what has just happened between us. Then I will ask leave to depart first thing in the morning. All I need really is one of those ships down there. Surely he can part with one; he's not sailing away again so soon, is he? Also a few hands for it; that Polybos and his friends will do. They are only going to make trouble for him anyway when the boy is fit again. Now the question is where should I say that I am heading?

(*After a little.*) Anywhere, nowhere, just so long as I get away from here.

(*Again a pause.*) I can feel the sea already, blue-misty, cool.

But it will be hot out there. Remember how raw-skinned they all are, he and his heroes.

Even so there will be a breeze. . . .One time long ago (I was around twelve years old) my special friend, the serving girl, went to Korinth with my father's steward to buy some cloth and things from a Sidonian ship there. On her return she told me about everything she had seen, how the strangers had almost bronze skins and their leader was a big tall one with a long square beard full of row upon row of spitcurls. Well, I could take my chances among such now. Indeed if they did me and mine no harm, in time I might even grow to savor living among them, which is a far cry from how I felt this morning, isn't it?

By the by I have almost forgotten about Aigisthos. After my husband agrees to my request, as why should he not, I will somehow find a way to send word to him. Maybe under the circumstances the captain will help out with one of his men. Polybos and the others will have to be notified and it will not be all that remarkable if one more of his men should leave the citadel at the same time. And then we will all meet down at the beach just before dawn.

So. What I have to do seems clear. (*She makes a movement as if to rise.*)

Only supposing (*She sits back again.*) that Agamemnon does not give me a chance to begin. Yes, maybe he will get anxious on seeing me again so soon after the fuss I made and think of reaching for something.

Why then I will have to try to set him at ease somehow and at once, won't I?

But won't he imagine then that I have come to—you know? And if he does, won't he then be—willing?

Well? I said that I would do it if I had to, didn't I? But then I keep forgetting that he is worn out. No, it will not come to that, I am sure of it. And I wonder what made me think of such a thing at a time like this anyway? Why it's almost as if— Do I desire then?

I don't think so; perhaps this morning after Aigisthos left, but not now. Besides, even if such were the case, surely I would never dream of him, my husband, of all people as someone to do it with.

What is it then? There is something, I feel.

(*After a while.*) Eh, it is not good. I was watching his captive's face when he and I got into the chariot, that is, before she put her hands up to her wound, and I saw the way her eyes followed him.

Am I jealous then? Is that it?

No, not really, just curious, that is all. I would like to know some things.

Such as?

Has he changed any in that respect and if so, how? In other words what does he do with her that he did not with me? And when is it different? Is it when he puts his phallus in and moves it or before? In fact is there now a before? On the other hand if he has not changed, was it really all right, and was I simply too young and inexperienced to appreciate it? Or does she find pleasing what was not and still would not be to me?

What am I doing? You know, I have a feeling that I dreamt all this up just now simply to— I am going. (*She rises and walks to the door quickly.*)

But before I do (*Pausing there.*) shouldn't I have something ready to say to him at the outset this time?

I should think so. (*A moment.*) Ah yes, I will ask him what he wants done with his captive (along with anything else he can think of) so that it will be seen to first thing in the morning and he can sleep late if he wants—something like that.

And then?

I will propose my scheme to him.

You know, he may refuse me after all. There may be some reason that I can't think of.

Why then there is this. (*Holding the knife before her.*) Yes. I feel better now—almost happy. (*Exit, the knife aligned with her wrist as before.*)

·

It was quiet in the corridor as she went along. The party must be over down below. Happily they have either passed out there or gone home.

Then, observing how dark it was save for the occasional pale-whitish haze of a lamp—it seems as if he and I are all alone here in the palace. But of course this wasn't so; the captain and the stewardess were about somewhere and probably some of the men of the garrison as well.

Nothing happened, and there appeared to be no movement within when she reached his door and tapped on it.

Now what? She touched it lightly with her fingertips and it swung open.

There was almost no light, which was not as she had expected it to be. Either the stewardess has forgotten about the lamps, or else she and the captain thought he would be going right to sleep, that is, after being—with me.

He was sitting as he had been in her chamber, and as then his eyes were on the hearth. Still he was aware of her entry, it seemed to her.

She took the other chair, and again her eyes sought the hearth too. The fire was older here, she observed, all pale-red-blue—even so, pleasant to look at.

It is like a handful of violets.

Good, that is a good sign, as they say. Now begin, but be gentle, do nothing hasty. . . .

"What—what are you planning to do with your captive?"

He did not answer at once. Then, on beginning to, he had to clear his throat. "She will be sent for tomorrow."

"I ask because if that is what you want, if you want her to come and stay here in the palace, you will have to make some provision for it."

"Yes."

Shall I pursue it further? I don't know. Let me wait a

little; maybe he will say something more. I should think that he would.

But he did not. Maybe I had better try something else. I can always come back to this later if I am at a loss.

"Was my sister well when your brother found her?"

"Yes."

But I knew that, at least so I heard from Nestor at Pylos. Anyway that is that apparently. What else?

Aha.

"Is everything all right downstairs? A while ago I thought I heard fighting."

"Everything is all right."

This is very trying, and do you know, I am beginning to think that he is doing it on purpose. But let me go on with it, something may yet work. In any case what choice do I have?

"Haven't you anything to ask me?"

He gave a shrug.

There, you see, and I wouldn't be surprised if he were enjoying it too. What shall I talk about now?

Perhaps Helen again.

"When did you see my sister last?"

"Before my brother sailed."

"Ah?"

"She was in the palace when we took it. That is when I saw her. Then my brother had her brought to his hut and then they left."

Nice, this is very nice, go on.

"That is all?"

He shot her a look, not understanding.

"All you saw of her?"

His eyes moved away again. "Yes."

I can't stand this anymore. If he won't talk, why—let us argue then!

"Tell me, I have always wondered, how did you come to choose me as a wife rather than her anyway?"

His body became rigid.

She went on. "You know, every now and then over these last ten years a very ugly thought has crossed my mind."

His breath stopped.

"Do you know what that was?"

He got up with a sigh and went to the bed and lay down.

She followed and stood over him. "It was that you planned it all, the marriages, Helen's abduction, the war, everything, and that you did it there and then in my father's woods. Is that so?"

He shifted a little.

"Well?"

Now he was very still.

"Did you?"

"Yes." It was almost a whisper.

So—I was right.

She went and found the chair again.

Right! . . .

It began slowly, as such things do—as when a fierce wind suddenly arises along the shore and two young fishermen in a small boat are driven out toward the sea, and each works his oars desperately, only one in this direction, the other in that, so that all their efforts go for nothing. Finally they both realize what is wrong and begin pulling together.

The tears came faster and faster, until her hands went limp in her lap, and sobbing, she let the knife fall.

•

I must stop it, and at once.

Except that I can't! (*With another sob.*) He planned it all beforehand, the matches, the marriages, everything, and just for the sake of the war—the gold.

Why am I so upset? (*Somewhat in control of herself.*) I suspected as much, didn't I?

But it is not the same as knowing it for certain. As I told Aigisthos, everything then becomes meaningless. And it is! My life, the children's—everything. (*She sobs again, louder.*)

I must try and stop.

Only I can't, I simply can't! (*Yet again, louder still.*) Eh, I'm just a weak woman. (*Nevertheless beginning to wipe her cheeks with her hands.*) Yes, in the end, after everything is said and done, that is all I am, the kind they mean when they say, men—what can you expect, she is only a woman. And the worst part of it is that there he is lying just a few steps from me, this villain of my life, and all I have to do is take the knife and get up and go over there, and now there is more reason than ever to—and here I sit wailing.

No, no more. (*She grasps the knife and rising, begins moving toward the bed.*) I will. I will do it!

•

It was just about lightless there now, the last of the embers glowing to ash, and she had to slide one foot in front of the other to avoid colliding with something.

What is he thinking, I wonder? Does he know what I am about?

I rather doubt it, for then he would be trying to prevent it or at least saying something, yes? He may not even hear me. . . .

At any moment she would be there. And when I am, I will be faced with the same old problem, how shall I do it?

It seems to me that I have two choices: to come down blindly with the knife and keep on with it again and again until—I don't know; or else to try to find a good place with my hand first, like under the ribs, and do it once or, if I hit a bone, twice.

Under the circumstances the first possibility is more

sensible, but I think that I would rather take my chances with the other.

Here—her forward leg had found the edge of the bed, and now both shins were resting against it.

He stirred. "It is late"—with what seemed like a yawn.

"Yes."

Now I must be quick about finding a place. She bent toward him.

"It was not always easy for me—either"—he.

She froze. What does he mean? Easy to—"What?"

"It was not my idea, everything."

What? Not his? "Whose was it then?"

"Odysseus; it was his."

Odysseus? Odysseus! But no, it is not possible; he is—No—"It cannot be!"

Still it must, or why would he have said it, what motive would he have?

But that Odysseus, not he, dreamed up everything. "It is simply hard to believe."

And that he, the elder son of Atreus (whom most people surnamed *the great*, so illustrious were his exploits), was capable of being swayed by that one, someone he could hardly have known well at the time? Not any easier.

"And yet—"

But has he nothing further to say?

Apparently not or he would be saying it, yes? Anyway what more is there? Surely you do not expect him to tell you that he is sorry now and ask you to forgive him and things like that, do you? . . .

But that Odysseus is the source of all my grief? I still can't—

Only—

She turned around, the knife handle slippery in her palm. The way seemed endless, but at length she sensed the wall before her and feeling around located the soft wood of the doorpost. Finally, the door open, she faced him again.

"You—you are nothing!"

•

Down, down. It is as if that dream of mine is coming to an end: the floor of the watchtower has finally given way and I am about to plummet, feet first, to earth. What can I do to save myself? Can I yet?

She came to a halt, at long last, in the courtyard.

Oh Aigisthos, that was no work for me. You realized it, why didn't I?

And how very foolish I have been. Of course you should have returned here this morning. You could have stayed hidden in my chamber all day and then dealt with my husband, and easily, when he appeared there this evening.

But how was I to know—no one figured it—that he and his men would turn up like that. I expected, and so did everyone else, that it would be as when he left, with him triumphantly galloping back here and the men smart and serious and alert following hard behind.

Still maybe it is not too late; maybe Aigisthos can still come here and do something.

But how can I send for him? Would the captain be willing to go? The stewardess? No, there is no one.

I could myself, I suppose. Of course I would have to sneak out of here and walk all the way, which is all right. But it would probably take me the better part of the night, and since there is not much of it left, I have a feeling, by the time we're ready to start back, my husband would be up and about and maybe strong again. In any case the captain would be close by then, and I must not forget about Elektra, who if nothing else will put them both on the alert.

We could let it be then and try to make a run for it to Korinth after all; and quite possibly, as Aigisthos said, Agamemnon would be glad to see it happen, especially after this night with me and in spite of whatever Elektra fills his ears with tomorrow. But I cannot count on that, no more than on his remaining as he is now and being unable, infuriated though he might be by our leaving and her telling, to go after us at once.

If only he were to feel sorry, which he does in a way, but I mean really sorry. Or else fall asleep and never—

What shall I—? Oh Hera! . . .

She looked up at the sky. Cold-black it was. Oh Hera, you are supposed to be there, but you are not. Nor are you anywhere else because you simply—are not.

And yet (seeing the stars all pale-gold and mauve and pink and white, like living eyes), there is something somewhere, I think. Only whatever it is has no name or voice or ear, and it is neither a mother or a daughter or anything else like that, and it does not seem to care about anyone or anything here.

And so the answer does not lie with it. I do not even owe it an accounting in this matter.

No, again and finally I—only I—have the answer. . . .

In the meanwhile some vaguely familiar sounds had begun in the great hall: a kind of intermittent swish, like a broom going, and now and then a hollow tap, as of pieces of wood knocking together. And all at once aware of them —it is probably the stewardess cleaning up in there, and the captain perhaps is giving her a hand.

She ambled over to the doorway to see. So it was. Pools of wine were everywhere, making the squid on the floor tiles look redder and the dolphins purplish; indeed even Atreus and the other noteworthies on the walls had come in for a dousing with it. The captain was busy piling the larger pieces of smashed tables and chairs together and his woman was sweeping up the rest—splinters, hunks of meat, crumbs.

"My queen?"—the stewardess, a little startled. He had caught sight of her just then too and was also staring.

Eh, now I have them thinking—the queen is not getting on with the king. Well, it is too late to worry about that; the damage is done already.

"I'm just out"—as she retreated back into the courtyard —"for some air."

It is weak, but what else was there to say?

"Can I do anything for you, my queen?"—the steward-ess, to her back.

"No, I think not."

Still, do you know what would be welcome now? A touch. Yes, one such as women give to their men and children and sometimes to one another as well. And it would be especially welcome from this one—remembering how smoothly her hands massaged but with firmness too after the bath.

"Are you sure, my queen? Perhaps something to eat? You did not—"

"No. Thank you." Later maybe, after it is all over, but not now.

Anyway it is comforting to have them around like this. It reminds me of this morning in the chariot.

Their work resumed. How lucky they are; all they have to do is finish here, perhaps not even that if it suits them. My husband wouldn't dare take it amiss if they were a little lazy; whom else does he have? Then they can go and do as they please. Yes, he will take her by the hand—filmy and cool it will be in his hot tough one—or else sling an arm around her shoulders or waist, this after they have disappeared from view—ah, the force of habit—and then they will go up to her room and lie down together, some-what spent, but free, utterly so until tomorrow. Yes, it is enviable, their lot. I almost wish—

In vain. And come to think of it, I'm not so sure that I would like to wait on others, though of course I would do it if I had to. Still not very willingly, and Aigisthos the same, if I am not mistaken.

I must return to the matter at hand and see if I can— At least let me think about it some more.

She strolled to the balustrade and gave a look at the solid blackness beyond, mindful of the ravine just below and the sea somewhere ahead in the distance. The time for talking is past. Besides, there was never really any chance for that to succeed. I did not know how; he, if he knew, would not. So there is no choice now; the thing must be done. And if that is the case it should be soon, for while it does not look like it yet, the sun is surely on its way, I can feel it.

I think that I can do it now, go up there and get the knife (she had lost it before while running). No matter, find it. Only something about the whole idea still troubles me, and that, I believe, has to do with using one.

Why? First of all and obviously because it reminds me of Aulis. But then I have also seen a lot of blood today already—the heifer, the boy Polybos, to say nothing of my imaginings—and I guess it has been too much for me.

Is there an alternative?

Not really. Poison is the only one that I can think of offhand, but I have no idea how to lay my hands on some. A diviner perhaps? No, there is no time to look for one now. So I will somehow or other have to overcome my aversion, won't I? . . .

The sounds behind her had ceased, she suddenly noticed. What are they up to now, the two of them?—turning to find out.

But it was dark there, and they were nowhere in sight. What happened to them? Did they leave without my being aware of it?

"We are finished, my queen"—he.

Ah, there they are—distinguishing their forms at the bottom of the stairs.

"Are you sure there is nothing we can do?"—his woman.

"Yes."

"Well then, goodnight."

"Goodnight."

They began ascending. . . .

I think that if I do it quickly, that is, go straight to his bed, pick a place on him at once, and put the knife in and then leave immediately, it will be all right. In that way I will not even have a chance to think about it.

So. I will stay here for a few moments more, until I am sure that those two are gone. Then I will begin retracing my steps.

I can remember when the knife fell. It was by a door under a lamp just before a turn. . . .

Now there was a curious idea, when one begins to reflect, to try to take a city so well defended (it was common knowledge, wasn't it?) and with so many able allies (that too, I believe). And everyone used to marvel at his cleverness, that Odysseus; indeed probably they always will.

There was no doubt he did possess it to a greater degree than most people (still does if he continues above the ground). Only now that I look back on everything, it was bound to be (at least in the early days) a gift with mixed blessings, not having been tempered by what they of my husband's circle term experience. For where had Odysseus been and what had he done before he came to us at Sparta? Nowhere, nothing—that is, unless one is willing to label as world-shaking accomplishment the occasional snatching of a few cows away from some kinglet on the scruffy-treed mainland adjacent to his dry rock of Ithaka.

At any event, leaving all of this aside—or perhaps one shouldn't, for surely my husband was aware of it at the outset—how did a nobody from nowhere like that manage to persuade him to go along with such an absurd scheme? Why Agamemnon seemed so self-contained that day when he showed up from here in his gold chariot, and that certainly must have been the first time they ever laid eyes on one another.

Could it be that something besides talk went on between them there in my father's woods? According to Aigisthos things like that happen between some men; there are those who enjoy doing such things with one another. At the temple, he told me, quite a few of them, even, it seems, after they have been given a woman and a hut to live in, keep on going back to the boys' house to take their pleasure. Could that be the explanation?

It is possible. But on second thought, no. No, it is close, but somehow that is not quite it.

Well, whatever it was—some kind of weakness for him seems to be the only way that I can put it—Odysseus with that brain of his must have discerned at once the possibility of something like it being kindled in him and lost no time in getting to work. . . .

It was silent all over. I can go now, I think.

She took a few steps forward. But then—here is another thought, and one that Aigisthos and I have never spoken of, though it must have crossed his mind at one time or another just as it did mine. Even if I do what I now intend to, we will still not be able to look forward to a lifetime together.

Why? Well, Orestes will be all for punishing me when he finds out about it—the foul father-murder, as Elektra doubtless will call it. Either that, or if he is reluctant to because of some feeling for me, almost everyone here and the rest of the world will egg him on to it, if for no other reason than their recognition of him as legitimate ruler.

And that probably being that for Aigisthos and me, I wonder if I ought to do nothing now and let things happen as they will in the morning.

I could even help them along some, at least where I am concerned, by being present in the great hall when Elektra appears and laughing in Agamemnon's face when he asks me if what she has said is true. That is bound to send him into a rage no matter how low he may feel from tonight.

As for Aigisthos, if his priestess doesn't refuse to part with him, then he will get a chance to use his spear. And since my husband will have with him the captain and some of the men of the garrison (eh, maybe they will have a new captain) when he goes to the temple to discuss the matter with her, it will be over in a—

But how foolish I am! Orestes will not hear tomorrow about this. And when he does he will not set out right away; he must gather men and ships first.

So there can be time for the two of us together, though assuredly not a whole lifetime. And that time, however brief it turns out to be—I want it, Aigisthos too.

"It is ours!"—as she began moving, hastily now, toward the staircase.

— *IX* —

The sky trickles black. It is a-gurgle like a brook. It is a black brook. Or so it seemed to the old watchman there where he lay on the ground near the ship.

That is, until his eyes came open all the way. "But it is night." And that is not the sky or a brook running—"but a fire crackling." Yes, it was right there before him, he saw, propping himself up on an elbow. "Must have fallen asleep."

Then it all returned in a rush. "My prize! Cheated! The captain, he cheated me!"

But what's the use? There is no one to hear me—unless those boys are still around here somewhere or the captive is awake over there.

By the by I hope they did not go sneaking in there during my—absence.

"Eh, who cares!"

He pulled himself up—"Oof, stiff"—and went a little way where it was darker. Wonder who made the fire—making his water there. Certainly nice of them whoever it was.

Finished, he started back to his place to continue with his

snooze. But then—"What is this?"—noticing something hard by the fire, a pouch and skin, it looked like. Someone must have dropped them, one of the returned ones' women maybe. So, her loss.

He went over and sat down there and put his hand in the pouch and—"Good, good meat"—stuffed his mouth. Then grasping the skin and tilting his head back, he squeezed a long stream into it—"Ah, like palace wine." Or else I am just very hungry and thirsty.

Soon full and needing to let it all settle down, he lay back.

What is she doing, the captive, that it is so quiet in there? Maybe she—while I— But no, of course not. For even if she had wanted to, where could she go, a stranger?

I have a good mind to get up and do just that myself after the way the captain treated me—"The king too." Imagine it, riding off like that and leaving me in the hands of that thieving toad! Why if nothing else he could have had me brought to the palace in one of those carts there and seen to it that I got a nice hot meal.

Yes, I really ought to show both of them. And he rose again as if he really would.

But there was the dark hull before him, and now—hah! Only so daring was it, this new idea, that for a moment or two he had all he could do just to draw a decent breath.

Well (finally), why not? That would certainly fix them but good.

He raised up his tunic. It did not look like much there, indeed it was only like a little twig, a dry one. But, lo, on his giving it a few hard rubs, it grew into a— Why it is a regular—! And there as of old shone a little crystal star.

So now I will go and get her with it, his captive.

"Har! Har! Zeus her with my steerhorn!"

Still it was not all that easy, climbing up in there. Twice

after stretching and getting hold of the edge with his finger-tips, he had to—eh, no muscle—let go of it again, which for some reason made him fall on his—"Ouch!"—where his ass still sizzled from the promontory. Then, when he managed to hang on and haul himself up, the thing had shriveled up into a little old twig again and he had to stay put there in the darkness for a while to get it in shape once more.

Finally, though, ready—"Heh-heh"—he began walking forward, toward where there seemed to be breathing. And as he did so, his wonderful vision of this morning came sailing back into his head—how he would go up to the palace at Mykenai and find Agamemnon there on his throne surrounded by his best men all feasting and drink-ing, and how they would set before him the crispy-brown meat with the hot-spicy juices and he would wash it all down with a cold goblet.

Then soon, his big toe coming into contact with flesh, he sank onto it, and just like that—"*Blup!*"—the thing was in.

Meanwhile a harper was singing about a great leap of flame—"*Bumpety-bumpety-bump*"—followed by many lesser ones—"*Bumpety-bumpety-bump.*" They were like the stars at night—"*Bumpety-bumpety-bump.*" All strive for but none achieves—"*Bump-bump-bump-bump*"—

But—

oh, yes—

they—

do! . . .

Pretty good, heh-heh. He lay still for a moment, then—"Yuf" (sleepy)—began rolling over.

But what's this? His hand had lighted on a big, almost huge, breast. *I don't remember seeing the captive with ones like this.*

And what is she doing with her tunic off anyway?

In fact (he felt around a little more) she seems to be that way, very roundish, all—

"Oh, no!" He jumped up. "No!"—reaching the side of the ship in a bound and the land in another. "My captive! My prize!". . .

His old wife, she lay there with her chest still going up and down. "Oh, thank you, Hera. Thank you."

"Where is she? Cheated again!"—he, thrashing around in some brush.

"Though you know"—she, sticking a leg up so that it would dry out good in there—"it wasn't all that I had hoped for. On the other hand don't be upset; it wasn't bad either."

It was like— Let me see. Like when you are swimming in the ocean and suddenly a big wave comes rushing toward you, and you expect to get a hard whack in the head from it, enough to send you under and maybe forever. But instead it washes right over you; and then afterward you find that you can see and hear and do everything else just as well as before. The only trouble is, you are a little whoozy from the scare it has given you.

•

Kassandra had long been gone. What, with that bone nearly hitting her in the eye in the afternoon and not knowing what to think later, on hearing hard breathings by the ship and feeling it rock a little, she had decided that maybe it would be wise to get away from there as soon as possible.

At first she did not fare too well, for in her fright she had plunged blindly into a wood and almost the next moment found herself knee-deep in a kind of runny slime. Then when she finally stopped to rest and tried to gauge by peering into the distance whether there was an end to this wasteland somewhere up ahead, something long and lithe and very cold had slid by her leg, and the result was that she had again mindlessly taken to her heels and then lost what little bearing she had had.

At last, though, the oozy stuff had begun to get lower. But then no sooner was there the feeling of a real solid bottom under foot than she had spotted a man not far ahead, a very large one, and it looked as if he were going to try to snatch her as she went by. And—oh, horrible!—he would push her down and drive his phallus into her just like that other in the temple that time. And—oh, more horrible yet!—again one would spurt into her what she did not want there and would be unable to do anything about.

Then thinking that maybe it was possible to get around him, she had begun to run, yes, just like that other time. Only on this occasion her would-be assailant was not alone; no, there were others, doubtless companions of his, not far off, she had immediately noted, and they were also waiting for her with their arms ready. So realizing that they, being many, were sure to catch up with her and when they did, it would be as with the girl in the next hut in the Greek camp, she had checked herself and holding back a sob turned around and begun walking toward them. In this way, she had reasoned, they will not injure me, only do it, which is unpleasant but after all endurable. Then maybe after a while one will turn out to have no stomach for the game and put an end to it as Agamemnon did.

Except that on getting a little closer, she had discovered—why they are not men at all, but trees! Olive trees—she was in a grove of them. And the sob dying in her breast, she had moved on.

Soon a road had appeared up ahead, and now that she had presumably put a little more distance between herself and the swamp and the cold scaly creatures in it, to say nothing of the panting thing on the beach—I must think of what to do.

But there is nothing, she decided almost at once, except

to continue along this road, which naturally leads to somewhere, if not Mykenai then some other place, and deal with situations as they arise. Of course it would be best if I could avoid Mykenai and other large towns if there are any, this in all likelihood being a night for celebration and carousal.

As for going to his citadel, should I happen on what looks like the way up there, it is pointless, I think, for he is probably dead or soon will be. Yes, most likely his wife and her man have either killed him by now or are about to. . . .

It was not very nice of him to leave me like that, all alone. . . .

But it is useless to hate him for it or be bitter about it; he will never know of it. . . .

The best thing for me to do is to see if I can find an old couple in an isolated place somewhere whose son did not return from the war or a woman who lost her husband in that way and has children to care for and try to persuade them to let me live there in exchange for doing chores of some kind. Then, when everything has settled down around here— But what will I do then?

I really don't know and can't think about it now; probably won't be able to until then—but especially not right now. For just then she had to make her water.

I can do it here in the road, I suppose; only with me on my haunches like that anyone coming along would have me at a real disadvantage.

She headed for cover.

The trick is to go in deep enough among the trees so as to be concealed from view but not so far as to lose sight of the precious road.

There—she had found a little dip. Now—having bent her knees all the way so that down there was very close to the ground.

I still feel uneasy about doing it out in the open like

this—yes, even though she had regularly when they were sailing down along Mysia and Lesbos; and during the wide crossing and all of the trouble that followed, she had squatted right there next to her pallet and in full view of everyone. I guess I miss home—picturing the little room next to her chamber and the drain in it. . . .

Where was I?—she adjusted her tunic and returned to the road.

Ah yes, what to do, keep going. . . .

Soon, a little further on—hungry. Only it was not as usual—I feel sick with it.

When did I eat last? Let me see—there were those fishes this morning, or was it yesterday; I can't remember anymore. Oh yes, I almost forgot. I had some meat this afternoon from that bone—feeling the sting on her cheek anew.

Not long after this—my back hurts, legs too. And then somewhat later—no more, I can't go on anymore, at least not just now. Must find someplace where I can sit down for a while and at once.

She went among the trees again and headed directly back into them. There, after a little way, she came upon a fence —must be a pen of some kind—and found a place where the reeds were loose and squeezed through to the other side. Ah—easing herself down to the ground. Good—leaning back against the soft sticks.

But now all at once—pain! Something like a lightning streak had shot through her between the hip bones. And she sat straight up and held herself round.

What could it have been? Is my bleeding-time coming on or what?—relaxing a little, though not much; there was an afterglow of soreness.

I'm not sure, when was the last one?

I can't remember: back home, sometime before the horse.

Then it is time, I think. Only (sensing that her breasts

and navel seemed a little more swollen than usual) it could also be a child beginning. Or maybe there was one and now it is no more.

Well, since I really don't know, let's assume for the sake of argument that it is my bleeding-time; what can I do for myself? There is only one thing, rest, sleep if possible. She settled back again and closed her eyes. I am weary enough to, that is for certain. And if that fierce pain does not come again, I will.

But now something stirred nearby. She opened her eyes —it was a sheep. The next moment quite a few were standing around her.

Then—"Halloo!"—a man's voice. "There's something in the fold."

"It's that cat again"—another.

Instantly she was up and back through the fence and running away with all her might.

"There he goes! Get him!"—from behind her.

"*Zip!*"—went an arrow or something by her head. She went even faster.

"*Zip!*" This one brushed her arm. Must— She reached the road and took off down it.

But no more of those things came flying, whatever they were. So giving a quick look round and finding not a soul there, she slowed to a hurrying walk.

Except that soon—can't anymore. She sank down and stretched herself out—let them come if they want to. Her eyelids fluttered and she would have dozed, only a dog barked somewhere. They blinked open once more, and she tried to rise. But no—falling back again. Can't, let them.

She focused her gaze on the heavens and kept it there, waiting. How deep-dark it is here, the sky. And the stars, they are so sharp.

It is like a black sail with pieces of glass stuck on it, silver, blue.

Yes, and something is shining a light there. . . .

Have I slept?—refocusing her eyes. It would appear so, for everything up there seemed stale now. She arose and set off once more.

The pain was back and steady now. It is like a headache, only down there. I hope it doesn't begin to bleed before I get inside someplace. If it does, I will keep my legs close together and hopefully no one will see.

How shall I proceed if I reach a town first and someone, some men—?

Ah, there is something now—on hearing sounds coming closer after she had progressed further. Soon there was a mud brick wall before her on her right, and inside—*"Tew-tew"*—pipes were tooting and *"Dub-dub"*—drums tapping and—*"Har! Har!"*—people, men mostly, making merry, and the air smelled of smoke.

It is like that night, that last night of Troy. . . .

After a while a wall like that appeared, this time on her left. Then there was another on her right, and so on, until finally they made a solid line on either side of her and the sky was reddish from the fire-glows within. This is Mykenai, I expect, but if not, it doesn't matter. I am almost sure that it is though.

As I said, it is not a good idea to linger in a crowded place like this tonight. And feeling better somehow, the ache still there but not as bothersome—used to it—and not even hungry anymore—maybe there will be a few solitary houses up ahead and I can find someone to let me spend the night at least.

Yes, but I will have to stay on the main road and there is bound to be a fork somewhere along here, perhaps more than one. How am I going to decide each time which way to go?

Maybe the clarity will come and help me then. . . .

Fortunately the way was clear, the air as she went along there resounding with merriment behind the walls.

Only—"Oh no!"—she had judged everything too hastily. For now there was trouble coming toward her in the form of two men obviously from the ships and reeling; that is, until—

"Say, Lykon, isn't that the king's captive?"

"So it is, Menon. Come on, let's get her."

Upon which they sort of began to run.

"Must—must think of something fast!"—she.

And she did. Just as they were there and thought to make a lunge for her, she burst forward, and each having kept close to the wall on his side to prevent her from slipping by, she did just that, only down the center and between them.

"Hahahahaha!"—from behind her.

Eh, they must have fallen down, the ass-faces. But she did not look round to see.

.

"Heeheeheeheehee!"

"Heroes, you're making too much noise, heroes"—from somewhere.

"Wha'? Whosat? Who said that?"—the one called Lykon.

"I did"—a woman, poking her head out of a gate.

They scrambled to their feet. "And who are you?"—he again, swayingly holding on to the other.

"My name is Helen. I am the widow of Epiarchos."

"Epiarchos?"

"Yes, did you know him?"

"No, never heard of him."

"I did; I knew him"—the other, Menon.

"You did not!"—Lykon, giving him a shove. "He didn't" —to her.

"He was in the ship commanded by Polynatos"—she. "It went down by Maleia."

"Ah"—Lykon.

"Say, do you have anything to eat in there?"—Menon.

"Yes, and you're welcome to it if you care to come in. But you must be quiet; there's an infant sleeping."

"Infant?"—Menon again.

"A child."

She stepped aside to let them pass. "There's a lamb tied up by the wall there"—it would have been her man's dinner. "If you will—" And while she stirred up the fire, they slaughtered and skinned it and spitted the meat with the sticks she gave them and set them to roast. Then she went into the house for another cup and chair, and the three of them sat and passed the carafe around, waiting.

"How about it, would you like a song?"—Lykon, after a little.

"Not really"—she.

And she meant it. No, all she wanted to do was cry as she had the whole day long, that is, ever since all sad-pink in her tunic she had seen the ships come in, but not her man's, and asked and learned. For he had been a good one, Epiarchos, the best—the teardrops beginning to well up again. Always took care of everything that needed it, mended the wall, fixed the cart; seldom if ever grumbled like others one hears about, and this even when she did something wrong and he had a right to, like that time when she drank off the milk that he had been saving oh-so-carefully to make cheese with. More than that every night no matter how tired he felt—and sometimes it was very, he put in a good hard day—he always used to do it to her and needless to say— Oh, Epiarchos, Epiarchos!—now they were about to overflow onto her cheeks. To think of how close you were.

Still—"Nsss!" (a sniff)—life must go on. So she had tried to make herself believe several times already today, first while trudging back alone from the ships, then later on sitting here by herself and watching the light fade. Now once more.

Yes, only there are problems, or rather there is one and that very very serious. For chinks in walls and limping cartwheels she could take care of, had in fact since he left. But that which he used to do with her every night tired or not was another matter. Indeed what with it throbbing down there almost all the time, especially at night, it had been a constant source of trouble for her.

And oh, the things that go through your head when it gets like that and your hand skips down there, then away, and then there again; no one would believe it. Like the prince Aigisthos, how small his is, I imagine; it must be very annoying to the queen. Why I wouldn't be surprised if she got him to do it with his tongue first. And then there is the captain's; his must be very large. Why it probably hurts the stewardess. But no-no, it wouldn't me!

One day a year or so ago she had reached the limit of her endurance and gone running out of the house and down the road to the end of the town, screaming almost. Then wandering droopily around in her man's pasture, she had come upon this youth lying under a tree and planting herself beside him, put her hand under his loincloth and given what he had there a little squeeze, then gotten on top of him and taken it into her. And for a while it had been fine. In fact she had just been on the point of asking him to—when he— Oh, but he was just a boy really. I'm not sure, it may even have been his first time. Then a little later when her hand had crept back there to try to—he had yawned and turned away from her.

And oh, you can't imagine what happened after that, such a stupid thing. Her bleeding-time hadn't—when it

should have, and then her breasts and belly had begun to—
Still life had gone on. And when it was born and had lived,
she, with Epiarchos due to return at any moment, had
begun trying to think of how to explain it.

But he hadn't after all and never would; no, nevermore
would she see him again. So now with herself all healed up
once more, now what?

Well, why not one of these here?

These? But the two of them together from what I can see
don't equal a poor Epiarchos.   ·

On the other hand it may not be as bad as it seems with
them. Perhaps it's just those rags they have on that make
them look like that. Anyway who else is there? You didn't
see a crowd loitering around in the road outside, did you?

So supposing that I were willing to consider it, which
one of them would I choose? For indeed the pair looked so
much alike they seemed like one person.

Well, we shall have to see, won't we?

She got up. "Here you, Menon, stay here and watch
everything, will you? I'm going to take your friend inside
and find him a fresh tunic. Then when we come back, I'll
do the same for you, all right?"

"All right"—he.

"And how is it that you're not at home?"—she, to
Lykon, as they walked along toward the house.

"I don't have any. When I got there, I found it burnt
down and everyone gone, I don't know where."

"Ah"—a few fingers on his arm. "And your companion?"

"His wife took up with his younger brother while we
were away, and he and his friends were waiting for him in
front of the house with clubs, and they told him to leave
and not come back again or else."

"So"—letting them fall to his thigh.

Inside now—"Here let me help you"—she, giving his
tunic a little tug at the neck; it came away in her hand.

Then scooping up his thing, she began to knead it. "Would you care to lie down for a while?"

"Yes."

She led him to the bed and stripping off her own tunic, drew him onto her. But—eh, not so good—on its going in. No, it wasn't as she had expected it to be.

What's wrong?

Aha.

She pushed up on his belly with her fist so that it came out again, then took it and began dabbing it around on her piece of flesh there. "Do you mind?"

"No."

Soon it began to feel better, and she put it back in. "Now go slowly and press down there"—wriggling round; the place was somewhere in between.

He did.

"Nice, very nice. Now go around here"—showing him once more.

Again he followed her, and again it was— But now she couldn't think about it, for now (a little, a little, a little more) and yes! And the next moment he too.

She let them lie there for a while. But presently—"We're forgetting about your friend." And she got up and brought him one of her man's tunics to put on.

As they went out—now this was not bad, that is, considering how long it's been for me, him too probably. But before I make up my mind definitely, let's see what the other has to offer. Not much, I'm willing to bet. Still you never can tell.

The two changed places. Then she, to Menon, as they walked along—"Your friend tells me that you have a wife."

"I did, but no more"—with a little grin.

Inside she would have—as with the other. But how nice —he took her round and put his mouth on hers and licked her lips. At the same time he made little circles on her breasts with his fingertips. So when their tunics were off and he was on top of her in the bed, it was not surprising to find that he knew how to go by himself, pressing here, there, rolling round, everything. And so it was over for her—ah —almost at once.

What now? She slung her legs over his back.

Interestingly, she noted (there was time to now), they seemed to fit together a little better than she and Lykon had. It has nothing to do with size really, she concluded. The two are both about the same there; in fact this one's is probably a little smaller—that is, shorter. Rather it's a matter of the flesh or bones above it or something like that.

In any event, soon, with him still moving, they were down and all tautened again, her legs, and her back was up in the air and her belly pushing against his, until—"Oh!" And at the same moment he too—"Oh!"

"Was that good, did you like that?"—she, after a little. "Yes."

Then she, after another pause—"I'm hungry, aren't you? The sticks must be done by now; let's go and eat."

"All right."

Well?—once they had done so and the three of them were handing round the carafe again. Which one is it going to be?

The answer is not as easy to arrive at as it might seem, for Lykon is more to my liking temperamentally, that is, he acts more like a man or as I think a man should, which comes down to the same thing. Still I can't help myself, I choose Menon. And who knows, maybe something will be with him in that respect too after he's away from the other for a time.

So what shall I do with Lykon, then?

Eh, I'll put him out to pasture. That is, she would send him to take over from the old one her husband had set to tend the sheep, he having grown somewhat feeble of late.

Then if and when things get dull around here, which hopefully they won't (at least not right away), why then—heh-heh—I'll pay him a little visit and see how he does, Lykon the shepherd.

.

I must have missed a fork—Kassandra, halting to rest. For the line of walls on either side of her came to an end just ahead and the road beyond seemed to swing upward, which probably meant that it led to the citadel.

Perhaps I ought to turn back and look for it?

No, I better not. I might meet those men again.

Why not try one of these houses here then?

It was an appealing possibility, as she was just about at the end of her strength and the ache down there had worsened—it was like a raw wound now.

Only chances are those just returned live in them, and they might want to—you know. Or else they will not take me in because they are afraid of their lord.

So I am to go to his citadel after all—she had begun to move forward again, but very slowly. Well, it is probably what I really wanted to do all along anyway.

And when I reach the gate up there, what then?

What else? I will tell the men that I want to see the queen.

But it is the midde of the night; surely they will not go and get her now, not even if they believe her still awake.

I will ask them to let me come in and lie 'down somewhere until it is light. Maybe that captain will be there; he seems very harsh, like Hektor and Deiphobos, but I suspect he isn't really. A little room in the garrison house will do, if not, then some straw in a corner of the stable.

And when I finally do see her, what will I say?

I'm not sure, let's see how she greets me first. I must admit, though, that she did not seem like a bad person down at the beach, unhappy perhaps, but not cruel.

Of course I will try to make it clear to her that the quarrel she had with her husband, whatever it was, is none of my affair and I have passed no judgment on what she and her man have done. . . .

You know, I am of about the same age, I think, as that elder daughter of hers.

.

The old soldier's granddaughter lay with her face buried in her arms—oh Hera, it has all gone wrong! And this was so not only as far as her returned father was concerned but everything else as well. Yes, nothing had turned out the way she had wanted it to that day.

It had all begun on her growing tired of her grandfather's silence. This was just after they had arrived at the beach.

Thinking to find it a little livelier elsewhere, she had slipped away to the next tree and a group of women there. But all they had talked about was cleaning the house, doing the wash, and things like that; so she had moved on again, back up the road.

Soon, going a little way, she had come upon a pasture where some youths were leaping over the cow of the sacrifice.

"Hey, that looks like fun!"—she. "Can I have a turn?"

But they had acted as if they had not heard her—and perhaps it was so—just brushed the damp locks out of their eyes and licked the salt from their lips and kept on sprinting and vaulting.

Oh well—and she had walked away.

Then, a little further on, she had spotted a bunch of boys behind some bushes with a she-goat they had gotten hold of.

"Oh, good!"—and she had run to join them.

But while they had not seemed to mind this, soon they had grown bored with just teasing the nanny and decided to play at a new game with her—to see who could put his thing into her rear first.

And she, well, she had hung around to find out who the winner would be, and after they had hoisted him up and his mouth had become all set and jaw tightened as he stuck it in there, she had decided to return to her grandfather and stare at the still empty water with him again.

Then while doing this, it had occurred to her that never in all her life would hers grow enough, no, no matter how much she might pull at it at night, which she did sometimes —so that I can get to win at that game.

Not only that, I have a feeling that there is a place down there where a boy, he can—in the same way.

At long last the ships had entered the bay, and it had been really nice watching the black hulls cutting paths of white foam as they made for the shore.

But then, when they had reached it, matters had taken a turn for the worse again. For on seeing the men jumping down with their hair all wild like that and without swords and spears, to say nothing of cuirasses and helmets and greaves, and noticing the old eyes next to her narrow a little as one of the strange ones had moved toward them—can it truly be he, she had wondered? And—as he had not been alone—what manner of creature is it that he leads along there? That is, it had seemed to be a woman—but why does her face have such a stupid look, and how is it that her mouth drips like a dog's muzzle after it has raised it from a well bucket?

"Her I won in the draw"—he, to the old one on coming up. "This"—jerking his head toward a foreign-looking carafe that she held pressed to her bosom—"I captured by myself."

"Ah."

"You the daughter?"—he, to her, his child.

"Yes."

Once they were all back here at home, things had gotten even worse if that were possible. Without further ado he had pulled the queer woman inside and drawn the curtain, so that she and the old one had no choice but to bed down here on the porch. And then—but oh Hera, it was horrible —his voice had boomed out—"Now you Trojan, you, I'm going to tear you apart!"—and a moment or two later there was an ear-piercing shriek.

Eh, she had concluded, shuddering a little in her corner, it is happening like with the goat.

Only his (with a wince) must be very large. . . .

Now although it was dark out and had grown quiet in there, save for a sob every now and then, the girl stuck her head even deeper in her arms—yes, to make it even darker and quieter. For nothing, but nothing, had gone right.

Hera, there is not even anything to look forward to anymore—sneaking up on a wild boar with him, rescuing him from a hissing snarling panther.

And her hot tears fell one-one-one. . . .

As for him, the old soldier, his shoulders were jumping a little too. To think that such a thing should happen to me; imagine it, to come back here after such a long time away without even a little bronze statuette to show for it.

And the worst part of it was that absolutely nothing could be done about it. For the person inside the house there was no longer the untried boy Agamemnon had taken along with him in preference to himself.

Eh, bad. And he shook some more.

But now all at once something new reached his ears, and it seemed to be coming from another house somewhere, perhaps the one across the way. It was a man's voice raised in anger and a woman whining in protest, and now— "*Whack!*"—and the woman gave a terrible cry.

So, they are catching it. Good, good for them.

"Stinking holes!"

•

I am here, I guess—Kassandra, with the wall and bastion before her on either side. The gate must be straight ahead somewhere—utter blackness there.

If only it did not hurt so. For now the ache down there was like a tearing, and so bad was it that she could barely put one foot in front of the other.

Also I think it has begun to bleed—sensing a sticky wetness on the inside of her thighs when they touched.

Well, it is just a little further. . . .

How fine it is here—now a part of the blackness herself and feeling a breeze at her back. There was a trace of melting sweetness in it, jasmine probably. It is almost like home.

Only now suddenly there were breathings nearby. Yes, breathings again! And either someone or a thing is lurking here somewhere, or I am—

But no, she would not try to think it through even. No—"Enough!" And tilting her head back so as to be sure she was heard—"Is anyone up there? Please, if you are—"

— X —

"Who is it? What do you want?"—a thin voice, from the bastion.

Ah, a young one; lucky.

"I am Kassandra of Troy. I would like to see the queen."

She heard him whispering up there, evidently consulting with someone. Then—"Everyone is asleep"—a different voice but smallish too.

Luck still holding; this one is also.

"But I must see her—at once. I have something important to tell her."

The low talking resumed.

Eh, it is forever the same with males, and no matter how old they are, it seems. They drone on and on, and then finally when their minds are made up, it is almost always too late.

Her ears detected a crunching, as of leather on pebbles. "I am going to get the captain"—the first one.

Better, feel better. And then, as the sound faded away, it began to be even more so with her, among other things because the breathings too had ceased. Must have been my imagination playing tricks on me.

You know, maybe for once the clarity was doing that

too. Yes, maybe she does not have another after all and Agamemnon is still alive.

Could it be?

Well, why not?

Then in that case they are together as before, however that was, and indeed it may not have been out of thoughtlessness at all that he left me before but rather because it would have been awkward having me around.

What will he do with me, how will he greet me then?

No matter, it is she I must worry about, and what I had better do and at the first opportunity is show her that I have no intention of taking him away from her or anything like that. And while I am about it, I should keep my eyes on the floor so that there will be no chance of meeting his.

There was crunching above again, but this time more of it. Then—"This is the captain. Now who is it down there?"

"It is I, the princess Kassandra."

"But what are you—? You were supposed to—"

Hm, did not give any thought to that, explaining my presence here. All right, let's see what he makes of this—

"Yes, captain, but the man you left to guard over me, he—he tried to—" Which may have been true for all she knew, though she was under the impression that he had been asleep when whatever it was had tried to huff and puff its way up into the ship.

"I am coming down."

And she heard leather begin to slap on stone.

Well, I'm almost there. In a few moments the captain will be leading me up to the palace and putting me into the hands of the chief servant (the grey woman, if I am not mistaken) and she will be finding me a place for the night and, who knows, maybe a few scraps left over from dinner.

Then as soon as it is light, she will rouse me and help me to dress, and bring me before them in the great hall,

Agamemnon and his queen; for of course the two of
them will be there side by side. And on hearing me out,
why they, kindly smiling, will grant me a house with a few
servants somewhere.

Or else, if it turns out that she, knowing or suspecting
about us, thinks herself unable to abide my presence in
the neighborhood, then let him send me home. Uncle Antenor and maybe some of the others are there somewhere.
Why they may already have begun clearing away the de-
bris. . . .

From just inside something went *"Clang."*

That is the bar being taken down. Yes—the doors were
beginning to creak.

But suddenly—"Oh! Oh no!" The clarity had come and
as never before, with an almost blinding light, and then,
scarcely the next moment, someone had grabbed her from
behind and was forcing her forward, a spear in his other
hand.

"Aie!"—one of the boys in the doorway, it sounded like,
as this one lashed out at him.

She struggled to get free, but in vain. Then all at once
pointy cold metal went into her under the chin, and feeling
herself being released now, she slid to the ground holding
the raw spot.

He who had seized her fought on, until—"Aie!"—this
opponent, the other boy apparently, also fell.

The captain, it seemed, was already on the ground. He
said a few words that she could not make out to their assailant, and then the latter went racing away, presumably
up into the palace.

Who could it have been, she wondered, feeling the air,
cool, sweet, in her throat?

But she had no time to try to analyze it, for now something warm and runny was there as well.

Oh my father, this too? What have I done to—? What? It is not right, my father. Don't you agree?

He did not answer. . . .

.

The captain had been woefully weary by the time he and his woman had finished there in the great hall. Is it always like this?—he had wondered as they had gone upstairs. Does she always work this hard? I never realized it. So that on reaching her room, he had not been sure what would be with him. Nor had he felt much better after they had gotten undressed and stretched out on the bed.

But then she had begun to—oh, what a nice one she is—press her fingers down along the edges of his spine, and what with that and the smell there (it was something different, new, like roses) he had soon known that it would be all right after all.

Whereupon putting his mouth on hers and then on each of her breasts, the tips, he had thought—this time it will be better, as I said. Then on creeping down her belly like that until the hairs at the end there tickled his nose—hah—and sliding his hand down into them, he had said to himself—yes, she will have a nice memory for a change. And then with her body becoming floppy all over and her heart beginning to pound away like a little fist, he had decided—it is time. And it will be, I will make it perfect, and we will remember, both of us, always.

And so it would have been. Only as his phallus went in there, he had found—well, it had felt a little different from usual, somehow like orange and red sparkles. So that before he had even been aware of what was happening—

He had done it again!

"Would—would you like to kill me?"—he, after a little. And for a while there he had really been alarmed, for she did not utter a sound.

But then all at once she—"Hahahahaha!"—with her

whole body, her belly, shaking. And he—so, so—truly relieved—"Hahahahaha!"

Nevertheless, he—"It will be all right again soon"—on
her finally ceasing.

Upon which she—"Hahahahaha!" And he—what else
could he do—"Hahahahaha!"

All the same it will be, he had told himself.

But then, just as he had begun to feel that it was time,
that knock had come at the door. And then having heard
his boy out—"What? Impossible!"—he had dragged himself up and grabbing for his tunic and sandals, whispered—
"I'll be right back."

What had happened after that, once he had found that it
was really she, the poor girl, was not altogether clear.

Oh yes, on the way down the bastion stairs one of his
sandalthongs had come undone and begun going "*flick-
flack*," and what with his being a little fuzzy in the head and
his boys descending before him—eh, he had thought, liable
to trip and break my neck if I'm not careful, theirs too,
hah.

Then below, while waiting for them to see to the bar, it
had struck him—this is very careless of me, going around
like this without even so much as a dagger at my side.

Still, he had reasoned, it is only a woman out there.

However, one should always be prepared even when
there appears to be no need, he had argued back. In that
way one decreases or maybe even eliminates altogether the
chances for a bad surprise turning into a worse one.

But then with the bar down and one of the boys about to
give the doors a nudge while the other held his spear—well,
it is a little silly for me to go and get something now. In the
future I will try to be more careful, I promise, yes, beginning tomorrow.

Only—oh Hera!—just then the doors had banged open,
and knowing only as the first boy went down that there was

something deadly to be dealt with, he had dived to the ground, hoping that the second would have sense enough to drop one of the spears, which he did. Except that just as his hand had come up with it and he was on one knee and about to rise to the other, a spearpoint had gone into his side and been yanked out again!

"You—you dared"—he, to his attacker, who had stood there by him for a few moments. Nor had he bothered to raise his eyes then, for by that time he had guessed who it was. Indeed who else could it have been? . . .

Now with himself still lying there and his hand still clutching the bad place—ah, the king is all alone above. For the two boys had been all that he had, his others having either gone off (with or without his leave) or else fallen down drunk somewhere. I should have—

But maybe I still can; yes, maybe it is not as serious as it seems. He gave himself a push up with the spear so that he half-sat.

But no, not ready for that—yet. He sank back again. Must have (with a deep breath) a little rest first. . . .

Meanwhile spring has come to the pine forest, and a thousand icy rivulets are running, spawn of mountain snow. And everywhere water is gurgling, or else swishing or trickling; it goes *"drip-drop"* from every bough. And things when they make a sound, like a twig snapping, echo wetly.

As I thought, a stag is there in the brush, a nice rich red-brown one like yesterday. And he is winter-thirsty, this one, and I should try to get him while he drinks. So where, oh where is it, my spear?

Only on reaching for it, his hand found hers.

But what is she doing here? You should not stay here, he wanted to tell her, as it cannot do you any good, all this dampness.

Except that it is all right, her hand assured him.

And it was so. For she was different from them, all the other women—like a soldier—and she will survive it and easily.

Still he wanted to go after that stag—he is as good as the other if not better. He tried to get up.

Only I am so tired—falling back. It has been a long day.

All right then (he drew another deep breath) I will let it go for this once.

But—"It will be better, much better, next time"—I promise. . . .

•

Bath-bath, in my bath. Here he is, the king, in his bath.

How did he get here? Walked of course. You did not expect me to sail, did you? Ho-ho, oh-no, no more ships for him, oh.

Yes, after she left, I took a little stroll for myself. And then here was this tub full of water, and trying it with my finger and finding it was just right, not too hot, I stepped into it. So now (squinting up at the light, all bluish-white) here I am, and it feels good, and—"Come and see me, everyone!"

No, no, I don't really mean that. No, don't do it— "Anyone!" . . .

She had the knife with her then, I know it. And if she had decided to go through with it, I don't think there was much that I could have done there in the dark like that. Why didn't she, I wonder? . . .

Oh Hera, I don't deserve to be punished for everything, do I? She should go after Odysseus, don't you think? He did most of it. Tell her. . . .

Eh, he had the mastery over me, that Odysseus. And it was almost from the moment we met.

Indeed in a certain sense it began then.

•

I had just returned from laying my poor father to rest and dealing with the malefactor, and I was all fluttery inside, as who would not have been in my position: to have become high-king of Mykenai almost overnight and at so tender an age. Tyndareos and his people, as I recall, came down to meet me at the gate, and with them was a whole troop of young men, other guest-friends of his, I soon learned. Then the old one and I having greeted one another, we were about to go up to the palace together when, lo, from somewhere among them there came—"Did you have a good trip, sir?"

The voice was clear and high-ringing, and my eyes discovered a face that seemed to match it. "Yes, quite"—having judged it likeable, and I exchanged a smile with him too, I believe.

The next morning, as I and Menelaos and his friend Palamedes (whom we found there) were on our way down to the stable, there he was before us in the courtyard. It almost seemed as if he were waiting for me. And now that I think about it, he was of course.

"They say there is fine hunting hereabouts, sir"—he.

I nodded, and he, as if having obtained my consent by this, walked along with us, informing me as we went of his name and where he hailed from.

At the stable, my brother electing to go with Palamedes in his chariot and he, the Ithakan, appearing to have nothing better to do, I invited him to come with me in mine.

The next day, although I had made no further arrangements with him, there he was in the courtyard again when we came out, and on his once more striking up a conversation that lasted until we reached the stable, I found it difficult not to ask him to join us this time too. And the day after that it was the same and the following one also, until without anything being said really, he regularly made four with us there in the woods.

One morning I and he became separated from my brother and his friend, and our spear and bow having brought down a large boar, we were relaxing for a few moments before starting to load it.

"Nice girls the king has, don't you think, sir?"—he, as he accepted the wineskin from me.

I certainly did, in fact had already made up my mind that Helen with her dowry to say nothing of looks was a near perfect match for me; and it was only a matter of time, a day or so at the most, before I went and spoke with Tyndareos about it. Menelaos and Palamedes, I thought, could fight it out over the other, Klytaimnestra. Still a little amused and also curious to see what he would say, the bold one—"And which of the beauties do you favor for me?"

At this his mouth grinned but not his eyes, I remember. "Why that depends on what your object is, doesn't it, sir?"

That was the beginning.

At first I was a little wary of it when he unfolded the whole plan to me, which took place some days later. But soon, in a few more, I thought better of it.

Nor were we to stop with Troy, he informed me, once I had. Indeed this was only the first step. "Who knows, maybe one day we will go even to the coasts of Egypt."

.

But it was such a wild improbable scheme, my son. How did he ever get you to agree to it? Did he have or obtain some kind of hold over you perhaps?

No. I don't know; I don't know how he did it.

What? Why what do you mean? Of course you do.

Please, Hera, I don't truly, except—

Yes?

Never before or since have I felt toward anyone—another man—as I did toward him.

Can you mean—?

No, not in that way; I never cared for that. Tried it once

with one of my father's pages; it was when I was very
young, scarcely more than a boy myself, and I only did it
really because there wasn't a suitable woman around at
the time. Anyway I didn't particularly fancy it, putting it in
the back there where the dirt is. Made him take it in his
mouth too, but that didn't please me either—his eyes staring up at me.

Well then, I don't understand.

Neither do I. All that I can tell you is that he was different from everyone else, all of the other men I knew.

How was that?

Well, for one thing he seemed to excel at everything he
tried his hand at, even spear throwing. In fact hard as it
may be to believe, considering among other things the
difference in our heights, he clearly did it as well as I, some
people might even say better.

And then?

And then he had a way with yarns; yes, no doubt about it
he could spin a good one. Why even now remembering
them, I can't help— The one about that follower of his who
did something or other, I forget what now, and nearly
brought the whole of Ithaka to grief because of it, now that
was very—"Har!" And that other about that woman—
what was her name?—it was even funnier. One day he had
gone raiding over on the mainland, and afterward, when all
of the people there had either been killed or run away and
he had their cattle, the queen, who was very fine-featured,
had tried every trick she could think of to make him remain
with her, and this was after he had done it to her against
her will—"Har! Har!"

What else?

That's it; that is all.

You mean he won you over just from that, from admiring him for those things?

I guess so. . . .Yes, after a while being near him, I began feeling, and this was especially true when we were in the company of others, that I could not bear to be away from him even for a moment. Yes, it became like a hunger—that is the only way I know how to describe it—an insatiable hunger. I was constantly afraid that I would miss something. . . .

Only Hera, that's enough, let me be now. Sleepy. "Yes" —sliding down almost to his chin and closing his eyes—"I could sleep now."

But don't worry (perching an arm on the edge), I'll be careful; won't drown. "No, not anymore."

Except that it is very warm here—"Sticky." He shifted slightly to one side. My cuirass, if only—"It is a little too" —at the throat.

A hand went there, a woman's, he sensed. Yes— "Loosen it."

She began to, or so it seemed, for it was getting better— "Can breathe." But—"Take care!" It had pinched him a little there.

Eh, I'll be glad when the war is over and I do not have to put it on. Had enough of the thing. . . .

Whose hand was it, I wonder? Should I open my eyes and see? She is still there, I think. Yes, I can still feel her presence.

All right, but not now. He made a little yawn. . . .

My captive, when we were going down along the coasts, afterwards in the woods she always used to—

"I sleep now.". . .

•

So, he is going—Klytaimnestra, all the same noting that his lips were still moving.

Even so it is done. And in the end it had not been all that difficult.

On the other hand she could never do such a thing again, she felt, no, no matter who the person was and what the circumstances.

Having returned to the corridor earlier, she had gotten hold of the knife again, as it happened, just a little way from his door. Then on having looked and not found him inside, she had gone on to the right for a space—where is he?—then begun trying to the left—where can he be? And then passing here, she had heard the telltale slap-on-slap of the tub and—ah.

At first, having entered, she had simply stood there watching and listening and trying to understand. Then finally it had come to her—he is ill. Yes, that must be it—for he had seemed pale and, except for his mouth, was still. Who knows, he may be very ill, even dying.

In which case why not let things happen as they will.

But no, I do not really know that he is one or the other. It would seem so; he looks it. But I cannot say it with any degree of certainty. So I must proceed. And she had grasped the knife more firmly in preparation for raising it.

But again there had been the problem of how, where.

Then her eyes happening to light on the pulse in the side of his neck—why not there? And so she had shifted the knife handle around so that the blade was between her thumb and forefinger and held it poised.

If I were he as we all knew him before and I were in as sorry a condition as he is now, I would not want to live anymore anyway.

This is more foolishness on my part. As I said, what I see may be only momentary. On the other hand, if it is not, I, not resembling him in the least, cannot possibly make any claim for this idea as an accurate representation of his feelings under such circumstances. Still it serves a purpose; it makes this moment tolerable, at least right now.

With this she had placed the point against the skin there and pressed down a little so that it slipped in.

For from this moment on I don't believe that I can ever look back on it with serenity, no matter what. And I will hardly forget it, I'm afraid. . . .

It is over now, I think—the blue-grey lips appearing to be shaping a final word. So now what?—about to turn away.

Well, now, Aigisthos; I suppose that I ought—

But she did not have to. Something in the doorway attracting her attention, she looked up, and there he was.

"I had to— I could not let you do it—alone"—he.

Besides running, he had apparently done some fighting and perhaps killing too; the tip of his spear seemed wet and discolored. "Yes"—she, vaguely.

"Where?"—with a motion of the spear. "Where is he?"

Her eyes fell.

"Oh"—he saw.

Then he came and stood beside her. . . .

So this is the man. But it does not look like him, no, not at all—remembering that one time he had seen him, when he was on his way to the war. Rather it looks—it looks like nothing. Only this is not so either, for obviously that grey oval is his head, and it lies at one end of a larger, reddish oval. . . .

He had not meant to return here; in fact the idea had not even crossed his mind so much as once that afternoon and evening. What had he done all that time? Well, to tell the truth not very much, just gone on lolling under that tree in the courtyard and continuing to sort of take stock of everything there, reacquainting himself with it all: the old grey-stone temple building where his mother had served, he too in a way from time to time—is she still above the earth, I wonder; the mud brick huts along either side of it, in one of which he and his father had dwelt; and the boys' house there to the left in the back—who could ever forget where it was—scene of the happiest days of his life before he found Klytaimnestra.

My friends are still here somewhere, I expect, naturally grown older like me. If I went around to the huts a little later, I would not be surprised if I happened on a few of them.

As a matter of fact before long I should go and find a place for myself there, as I may not hear from her until morning or even later.

And then there is the other possibility. I suppose that what I ought to do before anything else is prepare myself for it just in case. Upon which, having worked at it for a while, he had come up with this—

Obviously it would be better if she succeeded, for then we would have some more years together. But if she does not, while saddened, I will not be altogether so, as I will have the time just the same—that is, unless Agamemnon comes and makes Hera give me up to him. But even then all might not be lost, for with a little warning—say, while she is talking it over with him—I could try to make a run for it. To where will be a real problem, as no one hereabouts would dare take me in after today. No matter, I will solve it somehow or other when the time comes. The main thing is that regardless of the circumstances I will try to live for as long and as best as I can, naturally savoring as many moments as I can. If not, then savoring the trying.

It is not very good, he had decided in the end. But it will do for now.

Along about sunset there had come from a distance—

Aie, Aie, Aie
Aie, Aie, Aie

And the next moment the boys, who were all still down by
the stream, had sent up a shout and gone flying to their
house, where they had proceeded to—"Hoho! Heehee!
Hoohoo!"—and the like, that is, until—

> *Aie, Aie, Aie*
> *Aie, Aie, Aie*

the procession was near the gate. Whereupon it had grown
very quiet over there. Ah, the temple.

I ought to try to look for a place now, he had told himself, on seeing the priestesses and the girls after them go
inside and their boy drive the cart round to the back. Still
he had not moved.

I really should do something now, he had urged himself a
while later. For it was almost dark by then and little yellow
fires had begun to appear in the huts, meaning that the
men, some of them sure to be his friends, were back from
the groves and fields. But still he had done nothing.

Sometime afterward, just before the light had faded
completely, a serving girl had come out with a bowl for
him. Hm, temple food, always good, even when you are not
hungry, he had thought, and taken it from her. And his
fingers finding chunks of meat and nuts and barley there
seasoned with he did not know what—home!—he had de-
voured it.

Then he had leaned back and closed his eyes, thinking—
she will probably send for me later, Hera, if not tonight,
then tomorrow for certain. And if I am still here and can
do it, which probably I can, I will. If not, then I will beg off
with some excuse (I used to have a whole bunch of good
ones) and hopefully she will understand.

With this he had fallen asleep.

When next he looked around, it was totally black there,

all the hut fires having burned down apparently, and utterly still. How about a stroll, he had said to himself. And rising with a little hop, he had picked up his spear from the chariot, this to help him find his way to the gate and across the bridge, and set out.

He had not meant to go very far, just up the road a bit. Still the next thing he knew, there he was at the turn-off.

Better head back now, he had thought, on hearing it— "Har! Har!"—very much awake there in the town. All the same he had pushed on, passing straight through it.

Then with the last houses in sight—well, it is only a little further up to the gate, and what harm can it do? I will just go and stand there and listen for a while, that is all. You know, sometimes it is possible to learn a great deal from only a sound, even a tiny one.

But no sooner had he gotten there than—eh, what a stroke of luck when that girl Kassandra came along.

.

And now? Now having regarded this sad doing of his woman's for some moments, he was tired of it—she too, I imagine. So why don't we go down to her chamber and rest for a while. Then later, when she is refreshed, I will tell her about everything—the captain—which I am very sorry about. Was then, as soon as it happened, am even more so now, truly. He took her arm.

But they were not to leave just yet, indeed maybe not at all—ever. Having raised his eyes, he discovered Elektra there: she was standing in the doorway with a sword in her hand.

"So"—she, the weapon down but liable to be brought up at any moment.

His hand dropped, and he waited, the spear ready. When she sees what the tub holds (which she had not yet), only Hera knows what will be.

"So, you have come back"—she, moving a few steps toward them. Then her eyes widened, having found it. "Why—why you have—"

His grip tightened.

But she, she whom he cared for more than anything else in the world—"Please, no, it is my child."

Would you have her kill or maim us then?—he, with his eyes.

She put a hand out to the spear. "Please."

"My father, you have killed my father!"—the girl, coming closer.

So what should I—?

But there was no need to make a decision, for now the stewardess was there. About to pass by a moment before, she had, on looking in, seen and evidently understood everything at once. "No, princess, no!"—as she rushed forward.

Elektra appeared to have heard her but she took another step.

"Please, princess"—the woman beside her now.

She was on the point of advancing yet again, but wavered. Then all at once her face became wrinkled up, and—"My father!" (A howl.)

The woman drew an arm around her. "Come, my princess."

·

Elektra had not anticipated this turn of events; indeed it had been the furthest thing from her mind before, when she had almost hurried by the bath. But who could have figured it, that the dribbler would come back and do such a nasty unfair thing. And what made it worse, Her Foulness had gone along with it apparently in spite of the fact that it was her children's father.

All I can say now is wait, just wait till Orestes hears. For she would send word to him about it all at the first opportunity.

What had she expected to find? Well, for one thing Agamemnon alive; but it was a long story. Meanwhile the stupid tears were still running down her cheeks and the stewardess was continuing to lead her along the corridor toward the stairs. . . .

While waiting for the captain—the filthy traitor!—on the beach, in her mind she had carefully gone over everything that had passed there. Recalling that while her father had absolutely refused to listen to her, there had been no hesitation on his part when it came to that old one and his nonsense about seeing the ships first, she had been forced to admit that there was more to it all than met the eye.

Then, as she thought some more on the way home, it had occurred to her that maybe he already knew or suspected what she was going to tell him and did not care. Who knows, he may even be glad about it.

Yes, that must be it, she had concluded later, after having walked up and down with it for a while in her chamber. For he was caught, she had realized, in a difficult position: besides his wife he had that other there in the ship, and he was not as he used to be. And all he wanted, therefore, was for everything around here to return to normal as quickly and easily as possible.

So tonight he will probably do it to his wife, and tomorrow he will have the other brought here and at the same time send for Aigisthos; I don't see what else he can do. And then the two men having made it up—as why shouldn't they? Aigisthos only did as badly to him as he had received, if that, as I recall—the four of them would have a grand time of it, her father dribbling it into the new one every night and Aigisthos into Her Foulness again.

"But that must not be!" she had cried.

Except that it will unless something is done about it. Not

only that, it can get even worse. For with the two of them friendly like that it stands to reason that sooner or later they will want to exchange with one another—so that her father would be doing it to Her Foulness again and Aigisthos to the new one. And then having changed off like that once, what was to prevent them from doing it again and then again and again, so that the dribbles from them, the men, would be mixing in the women constantly.

"Oh, that is horrible!" she had wailed. I simply cannot let it happen.

And with this she had decided to go to him. Yes, as soon as it is quiet all over, she had said to herself, it having been very noisy downstairs just then, I will go to his chamber, and no matter if he has already begun to do it to her, he will just have to stop. Yes, I will pound on the door and shout that I must speak with him; he is to come out to the corridor at once. And when he does, I will say straight out that if that is how things are going to be around here, I do not consider him fit to be king anymore. Yes, in that case he is to step down from the throne immediately, and I—I will assume the reins of government. That is, until Orestes arrives, which will be soon; I am sending for him tonight.

As for the four of them, well, as far as I am concerned, they may do as they please, but not here, no, not in our citadel, Orestes' and mine. Yes, they must leave and the sooner the better, though tomorrow is early enough. They can have Argos if they wish. Diomedes will not return there anymore, I think, and they are free to do what they want with his wife.

And she had made for the door.

But then a cautionary thought had come to her—eh, he might not like this, my father. Whereupon she had set her course for the garrison house first, to find something there to add weight to her argument. . . .

About that time the stewardess had seen her. For when

the captain did not turn up after a while, she had risen and gone to find out what was keeping him. Then on seeing—ah—had sat down there by him to wait, what was about to happen being obvious.

What will be with me now?—she had wondered. How will I manage? For he had been a real help that night; indeed under the circumstances a steward could not have done better. And in the other matter, though it had not worked out—fatigue had prevented him from keeping his mind on it properly—he had tried harder than ever before, it seemed.

"I did not laugh at you with bad feelings, believe me"—she had said.

Did he hear me? I don't think so. He is very still.

Then, not long after that, someone who could only have been Elektra had gone down the ramp and emerged a few moments later from the garrison house with what appeared to be a weapon.

"Eh, the girl is interfering where one should not," she had murmured. The quarrel is between the king and Aigisthos, now that he is back, which clearly he is—there being no one else who could have caused all that grief there to her way of thinking.

And so she had made it her business to follow along behind the meddling one and try if possible to prevent her from pursuing whatever she was bent on. . . .

And now—"It is all the same again"—the girl. "Nothing has changed."

The two of them were just entering the great hall.

"You must be hungry, my princess." She deftly removed the sword from her hand and pushed her into a chair. "Let me go and see if I can find you something to eat."

Then tossing it—foolish thing—on the hearth, where there were some live coals still, she headed for the pantry.

It was a frightful mess in there, she and her man having

decided to leave that part for the morrow. But after rummaging around a bit, she came up with one of those nice little breads they had baked. Upon which, having smeared it with some honey from the pot and stuck it in a basket, she hurried back.

"I'm sorry, this is all there is, princess"—setting it in her lap.

"Yes"—the girl, eyeing the loaflet numbly. "It's all the same"—before picking it up and bringing it to her mouth.

As soon as she is done, the stewardess told herself, I will pack her off to her chamber, where hopefully she will do everyone a favor including herself—she has been up all night, it looks like—and go to sleep. Then—

But there are ever so many things to attend to, she suddenly realized. For besides setting the pantry to rights, she had to prepare the morning meal for those two above and the little girl, to say nothing of herself, and plan out the others for the day.

And then there is that poor soul down there. He, his body has to be seen to and before very long—noting with a glance toward the courtyard that it was nearly grey out and feeling the heat and almost fighting the flies already.

I suppose that I will have to do the same for his boys and the woman as well. One cannot just leave corpses lying around like that, can one?

That goes for the king too, no?

When will my girls show up, I wonder? In fact will they at all today, and if they don't, whatever will I do? . . .

Ah, Aigisthos, you have served me a bad turn this night.

— *XI* —

Klytaimnestra had tried to sleep, but in vain; Aigisthos the same. So after a while of lying there and somehow apart—was it because he had told her about the captain?—they had decided to go up to the watchtower and wait for the sun.

Now there she gazed at the pine forest, which was still black, then at everything else—the countryside, the citadel walls—all sleeping-blue. His eyes followed hers listlessly.

"What will be with Elektra, do you think?"—he, after a little.

She sighed. "Oh, she will be worse than ever now, I expect."

"And can nothing be done?"

"I rather doubt it." No, they would go on trying of course and perhaps end by keeping the little one away from her, but as before with Orestes it would be to no avail. Indeed Elektra would go on despising them even after they were gone—"until her own death, it would not surprise me."

In the meanwhile, hiding the real reason from everyone

but worst of all from herself, the girl would avoid them as much as possible as of old and again live only for that morning when yellow fires twinkled along the mountain tops announcing that black specks were in the gulf again. Upon which, when that day came, she would declare, gazing rapturously at it all from the bastion—"At last, at last justice will be done!"

"For he will come, my son, Orestes."

She turned toward the bay now, he with her; it was still all misty there.

Yes, one day soon—"there is no telling when exactly, except that it will not be long, in a year or two or five at the most"—the dark hulls would come gliding in, "just as they did today—"

"Yesterday."

"Yes"—and they would be full of young men all eager-eyed and glad-cheeked, the pride of Phokis, the special friends Orestes and Pylades at their head. And on the shore waiting to join them would be a whole host of others from here, these for the most part grown men with long memories of the plain before Troy and Agamemnon, stern but fair, leading the way. One could almost hear them—"Hail, Orestes!"

Then someone having thought to bring along a cow and some wine—"maybe your priestess will grace the occasion" (though more than likely she would want to know how matters stood first before venturing from behind her walls) —they would send its soul to Hera, vowing vengeance and to restore right rule.

And then they would all move up the road together, some in chariots, others carts, and still others on foot at a run—an expedition. But because the foreigners were green and the others at home, they would not get into any mischief along the way—"well, not much." Maybe jeer at some old one hollering out of his gate for them to leave his sheep alone, knock him down too; surely drag in among the trees any lone girl or boy happening by because—"Ah, it couldn't be helped."

Finally reaching the town, they would become wisely silent and quickly make for here.

"I will fight them"—he.

"Of course." And it would not be alone either. "I am thinking of a young man named Polybos; I will tell you about him later. And he has friends, that one." Also by that time there would be a new garrison here with a new captain over them, who with a little patient searching could be found and would remain loyal if treated reasonably well.

"I had best begin looking right away"—he.

She nodded.

"And we will be waiting for them with swords and spears and bows"—he.

"Yes, but all the same you will lose, I'm afraid."

He did not understand.

"It will be a matter of numbers, that is all. There will simply be too many of them for you."

"Don't be so sure of that. Maybe if I—"

"You will"—she. "You will try everything possible, but in the end it will not matter."

Yes, it would be as of old there with besiegers. While some fell to worrying the bastion and walls, the rest would proceed to get at the gates, rolling up carts laden with good dry twigs and setting fire to it all, then at the right moment staving them in, the smouldering timbers. And then they would all go pouring through three-four-five abreast, as many as the doorposts would allow, and push the defenders —"slowly to be sure, still doing it"—up the ramp and the staircase.

"It will end in the courtyard."

He scanned it gloomily.

She continued. "You and yours will back in there, Orestes and his right behind you. And then yours will begin to fall, until only you and I are left."

The next part was far from amusing; still curiously she found herself tickled by it and had to make an effort not to laugh. "You will be in front of me, protecting me, so you will be first. Shall I watch when Orestes, he—?"

He considered. Then—"No, that is, if you are right about all of this."

"Then my turn will come."

"Yes."

She went on to finish it, this sad part of their history. "Later on in the great hall, after they have all eaten and drunk their fill, someone will lead in an old blind one and he will sing about everything of note that has taken place that day, naturally as Orestes and Elektra and doubtless the others too will want to hear it." And while it was possible that he, her son, would experience some uneasy moments over it now and then—"that is how the whole thing will be received forever and ever, whatever that means."

He shrugged.

"You don't mind?"—she.

He smiled without smiling. "There is nothing much that one could do about it if one did, is there?"

It had gotten considerably lighter in the meanwhile, they both observed. Yes, the sun was definitely on its way. . . .

Down by the gate, where four dark shadows lay, two grey figures soon appeared, the stewardess and one of her girls, it looked like. They went to either end of one of the shadows (that which in all likelihood used to be her man) and began lugging it toward a little room close by. But after a few steps they halted and set it down, the task having proved to be too much for them apparently.

"Should I go and give them a hand, do you think?"—he, as if he would.

"No. Leave her. She would not want it. No, not from you. At least not now."

Meanwhile the two had taken up their burden again, and although it sagged in the middle, probably they would succeed this time.

Then, she supposed, they would return for the others and afterward bring down to join them that which lay in the tub above.

Later on, when it was fully light out and perhaps more of the girls and a few of the old ones turned up—"I have a feeling that some of them are asleep there in the garrison house and have been so since early last evening"—the stewardess would see to it that all four were suitably made ready and loaded onto carts. And then she in the lead one, Elektra following separately with her father—"though this I am not sure about; she may very well not care to take part"—they would go rolling out the gate and down the road a way.

There at a certain place the men would jump down and at the stewardess' direction prod around with spades until they located two chambers. Then, after pulling away the stones from their openings and going within and brushing aside whatever lay scattered about, old bones mostly, they would carry in and fold into some large urns the bodies of the two boys and that of the unfortunate stranger. And then, with this done, they would spread fresh mats on the floor and come and set on one of them the captain in his boar's tusk helmet, bronze cuirass and greaves, and on the other the king in a fresh white tunic.

Whereupon the stewardess, after signing for everyone to leave, would stand and gaze down at her former man for a while, then suddenly drop a little clay Hera on his chest and rush out. And the next moment the two places would be sealed up and packed with earth again. . . .

Aigisthos sighed. "Happily, if you are right, we will miss that, one of us doing that for the other."

"And a good deal else that is unpleasant too"—she, reminding themselves of the possibilities: feebleness, illness, perhaps pain with it. "So that in the end we are really—"

But now all at once there was a fine warmth on their backs, and turning toward the mountains and their hollow, they saw that it was glowing there. At any moment now.

"Yes, look!"—he.

For, lo, the sun was there, and now the pine forest was almost green and the land all over pink and full of little yellow flecks.

"It is like a motherbird"—she. "A great golden motherbird feathering her young in the nest!"

"If you wish."

She leaned toward him—it is all that we have besides one another.

He found her hand—it is enough.

NANCY BOGEN, a native New Yorker, is a professor of English literature at the College of Staten Island. Her facsimile edition with a new interpretation of William Blake's *Book of Thel* was named to the Scholar's Library of the Modern Language Association. The idea for *Klytaimnestra, Who Stayed at Home* arose out of an interdisciplinary course entitled *The Greeks,* which she taught at Richmond College with historian Phyllis Roberts. The background research was undertaken with the aid of a CUNY Faculty Research Grant.

Designer: Cynthia Krupat
Copy Editor: Raymond Donnell
Cover Illustrator: Alan Henderson
Proofreader: Sidney Green
Typist: Judith McCusker